C000053403

CRAVEN'S WAR
TO HELL AND BACK

NICK S. THOMAS

Copyright © 2022 Nick S. Thomas

All rights reserved.

ISBN: 979-8355126490

PROLOGUE

The third and most ambitious French invasion of Portugal seemed unstoppable after the disastrous Anglo Portuguese defeats at Ciudad Rodrigo and Almeida. Not even a brilliantly executed defence on the heights of Bussaco could stop the relentless French march to Lisbon, led by one of Napoleon's finest Generals, Marshal Masséna.

Yet the retreat to Lisbon was not to be another Corunna, where the British Army was forced to take to the sea and flee the country. As the Anglo Portuguese army retreated to the capitol with tens of thousands of Portuguese refugees, all hope seemed lost until they got to witness Wellington's preparations for themselves. For almost a year before almost every able-bodied man and woman of the region had slogged to build the greatest defensive line in history; three astonishing defensive lines bristling with cannons and tens of thousands of troops behind near impregnable defences. The slopes of hills dug out to make unscalable positions and murderous approaches. Such a sight brought tears to both sides, of joy to the retreating Anglo Portuguese army, and of disbelief and distress to the advancing French forces. The Lines of Torres Vedras were so robust that a preliminary attack was all that Marshal Masséna needed to see before withdrawing to await reinforcement.

But the magnificent defensive lines around Lisbon were far from the only obstacle facing Masséna and his vast army, for a scorched earth policy had left little food and shelter for the troops and their animals to survive a bitter winter. A long wait has begun, as Masséna waits for additional support from Napoleon, and Wellington bides his time, waiting for the perfect moment to lash out from behind the Lines of Torres Vedras.

CHAPTER 1

9th January 1811.

"Wait here." Craven handed the reins of his horse to Moxy, who he was leaving in charge for a few moments.

"And if you need the best shot in the army?" Moxy smiled at him.

"If we need rifles here, we are already in far more trouble than we can handle," replied Craven wearily as he looked around suspiciously, as if expecting to be set upon by the enemy at any moment. They were all on edge.

Craven could see Moxy's breath condense into a cloud of fog as it met with the brisk morning air. The ground was damp and only their greatcoats kept them warm, their rosy cheeks red from the bitter morning air. Yet it was a welcome reprieve from the packed and pungent lines of Torres Vedras and the vast Portuguese population of refugees and British and Portuguese soldiers which were contained within them, sheltering from the

French invaders and from one of the most bitter winters to ever strike the region.

"Just be thankful for these coats, as its more than many of those French bastards have got."

"It's hard to feel sorry for an invading army," replied Moxy as he shivered a little.

Craven smiled.

"How were you born in Wales with all that cold and rain and never became accustomed to it?" Craven laughed.

"I was smart enough to not be out in it long enough. Only a bad hunter goes cold and hungry."

Craven nodded in appreciation, as he didn't much like suffering hardship for anyone's benefit and would far rather have his feet up beside a fire and a glass of wine in hand.

"They've really made soldiers of us, haven't they?"

"We were dragged into this war kicking and screaming, but yes, they have."

"It was your idea to come here." Matthys stepped up beside them.

"For an adventure, not a war."

"I'm not sure I believe that anymore," smirked Moxy.

"You think I wanted all of this?" Craven sounded surprised.

"Yes, even if you didn't know it back then. You take to war like I handle a rifle," replied the Welshman without hesitation.

Craven looked to Matthys for a second opinion, but no words needed to be spoken as it was in the Sergeant's eyes.

"Well…" stuttered Craven as he was dumbfounded.

"Is it so much a surprise that a man who most enjoys

fighting and taking risks is born so naturally to war?"

But still he had no answers as he dwelled on the thought.

"There is no need to hide from it. We all have our calling."

"You had the calling of God, and yet here you are with us," smiled Moxy.

"A calling to look after his flock."

"And that involves fighting and killing?" Moxy pressed in a way he had many times before, never being satisfied with the answer.

"There has always been war, but it is for the righteous and faithful to ensure the right people win."

"I am pretty sure plenty who wear French uniforms say the same," replied Craven.

"Yes, and just as in the judicial combat of the ancients, God is on the side of the victor. When we win this war, we will all be vindicated and forgiven for the blood we have spilled."

Moxy opened his mouth to speak, but Craven shook his head to stop him. Neither of them understood the Sergeant's motivations, but it was hard to argue with the value he held to them all. Matthys smiled as he climbed up a shallow slope and lay down at the top. Moxy looked frustrated, as if he had been stopped from winning an argument.

"Let him believe what he wants so long as he has your back," declared Craven.

"And if those beliefs are mad?"

"We are all mad. Why else would we be out here in the freezing cold, earning a beggar's wage to risk getting our heads shot off?"

"Because it beats working endless hours in a factory?" he replied cynically.

Craven smiled and nodded in agreement before following on after Matthys and scrambling up to the vantage point where they could look down upon the enemy. There was a village ahead of them with French troops pacing back and forth.

"That's it." Craven pulled out a map to confirm it, the city they beheld, "Santarem."

Paget rushed up beside them to see for himself. "It's not much of a siege, Sir, thirty miles away from our lines."

"What would be the point in laying siege to that fortress Wellington has built?"

"They can't starve us out whilst the Navy controls the seas, and what good would it do to stand in front of our guns?" replied Matthys.

"Then what, Sir? What do they do here?" Paget asked.

"They wait."

"For what, Sir?"

"Everything. Reinforcements, food, powder, and for spring."

"What can he not achieve with more than sixty thousand troops?" Paget gasped.

"Masséna may have marched into Portugal with that number, but every day since has cost him dearly," replied Matthys.

"Bussaco lost them what, a few thousand?"

"And starvation and desertion a great deal more," admitted Craven.

Paget could hardly believe it, as either prospect seemed unfathomable to him.

"How could such weak-willed men ever have conquered so much of Europe?"

Craven laughed at his response, which sounded so disgusted.

"What is it, Sir?"

"You think our men wouldn't do the same? It's easy to judge others when you have a full belly and a warm bed at night, and you don't face the prospect of certain death in such a pointless assault as might yet still come."

"You think you would break, Sir?"

"There is only so much any man can take. I've seen good men reduced to nothing by such hardships, and I have come close to it myself." He was reminded of the horrendous retreat to Corunna.

"What are we doing here?" Matthys asked, concerned about the sizeable enemy presence before them and the modest scouting they had at their disposal; comprising of just fifteen troops, which was enough to protect from any pickets, but not nearly enough for a serious fight.

"We didn't come all this way for nothing," growled Birback as he hovered over them, enviously looking out towards anything the enemy might have that he did not, despite the shortages they were experiencing.

Craven sighed as he took out his spyglass and took a closer look.

"Look at them. Emaciated, angry, and as hard as stone."

"And just as brittle," smiled Birback.

"Don't underestimate desperate and hungry men," replied Matthys.

"At Antioch a starving army of crusaders, barely even able to stand, like an army of the dead storming forth, and they would not be stopped by any weight of arrows nor even the burning ground beneath their feet. I would never wish to cross swords with such men," warned Paget.

"Should we concern ourselves with what men did a thousand years ago?" growled Birback.

"If you don't want to repeat their mistakes, yes," insisted Craven.

The Scotsman grumbled but said nothing more, clearly feeling out of his depth.

"Look at them, that is a beaten army. Every day that goes by they are weaker, and we are stronger. We must wait them out a little longer," concluded Craven.

"What on Earth is that?"

Paget drew their attention to the West. A troop of thirty or more cavalry approached one of the enemy held villages.

"Enemy?" Craven lifted his spyglass for a better look and could tell right away that they were Portuguese cavalrymen. Their dark navy-blue uniforms were a pale and cheap looking imitation of those worn by the always-fashionable cavalrymen of the British and French armies. Their horses looked as emaciated as the French troops they advanced towards. Some of the cavalrymen wore cloaks and coats of no uniform type in an attempt to survive the winter whilst others had none at all.

"What do they hope to achieve, Sir?"

Craven shook his head in astonishment and continued to study the advancing force, when he realised the officer and several beside him were dressed differently. British greatcoats covered their backs and concealed the redcoats beneath, and he soon fixated on the officer as his face tightened into a frown.

"Hawkshaw," he seethed.

"What the devil is he doing out here?" Paget asked.

"Can't you see? He is trying to emulate his famous brother and earn such acclaim," replied Matthys.

"Brother?" Moxy smiled.

"Half-brother," scowled Craven.

It was clear most if not all of them already knew as Moxy toyed with him.

"Emulate me how?" Craven demanded.

"Your acts of daring," replied Matthys.

"He advances across open ground in daylight against a dangerous and numerically superior foe, how is that like me?"

Matthys shrugged as if not wanting to answer the question, knowing Craven would not appreciate his answer. Craven went back to his spyglass.

"A bloody fool," he scowled again.

"He's going to get himself killed, a problem off your back," declared Birback coldly.

Craven smirked and nodded in agreement.

"Surely you can't let your own brother ride to his death?"

"Mr Paget, you are talking of a man whose sole purpose of being here is to try and kill me?"

They watched as the small body of cavalry drew swords and advanced on the French held village. Two musket shots rang out from pickets, shooting one Portuguese cavalryman from his saddle as they reached the gallop. The musket fire echoed out across the rolling hills for all to hear for miles around, inevitably alerting many of the French forces billeted in the area.

Craven continued to watch as Hawkshaw stormed into the village at the head of his small force. He carried his sword high and rode at the enemy without fear, as panicked troops rushed out from every building to meet them. He hacked down at one after the other with both skill and ferocity and no fear at all.

"He's got guts, I'd say that for him," admitted Moxy.

"Getting more done this day than we are," groaned Birback as if jealous he was not the one wielding the sabre.

"Sir! Look!" Paget directed Craven to the scene he was witnessing with his own spyglass, but they could all see well enough with the naked eye to what he referred to. A large body of French cavalry was rushing towards the same village Hawkshaw was attacking.

"They must have heard the shots," said Moxy.

Craven looked back to the village. Hawkshaw was waving his sabre about his head in a whirlwind of excitement as he kept on the assault. Craven shook his head.

"What a fool he is!"

"What will we do, Sir?"

"Nothing, may he learn some valuable lessons here today," replied Craven with no compassion at all.

"Dead men learn no lessons," seethed Matthys.

"And so what would you have me do?" Craven demanded angrily.

"Whatever you feel for that man, he is your brother, and even if that still means nothing, he is a brother in arms."

But Craven would not budge, with such fury and fire within his eyes, and yet Matthys was not ready to give up. He leaned in and whispered to him.

"James, I have seen you kill men by accident and because you had no choice, and I could forgive it in time, but if you let the Lieutenant die, it will be neither an accident nor lack of choice."

Craven sighed in frustration.

"I will not ride with a man who would leave his fellow soldiers to die when he had the power to act."

Craven's expression of anger turned to one of astonishment, and he looked into the Sergeant's face to see he wholeheartedly meant it. As much as Craven disliked it, he could not ignore the words of the best man he knew.

"Mount up and be ready to fight!"

Birback smirked as he rushed back to the horses, eager to join the fight as Craven went ahead reluctantly.

"You won't regret it, Sir!" Paget cried enthusiastically.

Craven smiled as he shook his head.

"He is insufferable, is he not?" Charlie asked with a smirk.

Craven looked out at the tiny force he commanded. It was nothing more than a small scouting party.

"We get as many out alive as we can, nothing more. I didn't come here for a stand-up fight, do you hear me?"

But he could see many of them merely nodded along without even considering his words. It had been a long and bitter winter even for those well supplied behind their vast defensive lines. Most of them were eager to anything to break the monotony, even if it involved risking their lives. Craven dug in his heels and led them on. They soon crested the top and got a view out to the village beyond the rolling hills before them.

"They'll make it before we do!" Matthys pointed to the enemy cavalry who rode on towards the village in a frenzy, circling their sabres about their heads.

Craven spurred his horse on as fast as it would take him, forcing them to ride on without any weapons drawn. They held on with both hands to the galloping warhorses who seemed as eager to be set free as the soldiers in their saddles. Finally, they came over the last obstacle to give them line of sight to the village, just in time to see the French cavalry soar in amongst the British and Portuguese party. The scene erupted into a chaotic melee spread out across several streets. French infantrymen, emboldened by the cavalry who had come to relieve them, now rushed out from their hiding places with muskets, bayonets, and swords in hand.

Yet the poorly equipped Portuguese cavalrymen fought like lions, only matched by the ferocity of the emaciated French troops who seemed to come at them like demons. Three cavalrymen immediately targeted Hawkshaw and singled him out as they sought revenge and glory, but they were countered by his fine skills. He ducked away from the cut of the first cavalryman and returned a blow to the back of his attacker's neck as he rode past, causing him to slump over the saddle as the horse fled.

Another came at him giving point with sabre, but Hawkshaw cut down against the blade, battering it out of the way before plunging his own sabre into the man's chest. But for all of his success, others were not so lucky. A bayonet was thrust up into the flank of one of his comrades, and a devastating sabre blow came down on the head of one of the Portuguese troops. Hawkshaw looked around in desperation at how quickly the situation had deteriorated. Just a moment before, the Frenchmen who held the town cowered in fear as he and his men ran rampant, and now there were Frenchmen running amok, completely surrounding them.

"We can't win this!" cried one of his comrades.

"Retreat, retreat!" He pressed his force forward and tried to force his way out of the chaotic melee. He forced his horse to push on through several infantry and cavalrymen. He seemed to be making progress when he was forced to angle his body to the left and parry a cut coming for his exposed left side. His nimble blade got in position just in time with the point directed towards the ground and his hilt high in a hanging position. He was glad to have made the defence and made no attempt at a riposte as he pressed on. But as he twisted back into his natural riding position, he caught a glimpse of a musket butt swinging towards his head. He had just enough time to lift his sword arm, and have it bear the brunt of the blow, which launched him off the back of his horse. He crashed down into soft mud, the morning frost churned up by horses. It at least softened the blow, but still he felt the wind knocked out him. He looked up as the same musket stock came down at him like an executioner's axe. He placed his sword across his body and head, bracing it with his left.

The thunderous blow caused him to feel the blunt cold steel of the back of his sabre, but it was enough to save him, although the frenzied Frenchmen merely rained down blow after blow against him. Hawkshaw was weakened with each one but finally saw his moment to strike. As the man rose up for an even stronger blow, he quickly thrust into the man's thigh, and he cried out in pain. Yet with seemingly superhuman strength and resilience, he lifted the musket for yet another blow, but before it could descend, he was struck by a horse at the gallop and flattened.

Hawkshaw seized his moment to leap back to his feet, just in time to see his saviour bring his horse about. Hawkshaw looked furious at recognising Craven's face, but the Captain did not even meet his glance. He continued to strike back and forth with as much precision and ferocity, cutting and thrusting down several Frenchmen.

The scene before them was one of complete chaos as friend and foe were scattered more like a brawl than a battle. Paget galloped up to Hawkshaw, leading his horse up to him.

"Let's go!" yelled the young Lieutenant.

"You didn't have to come. I didn't need you!" he growled.

"No, we didn't, and the Captain wouldn't have," snapped Paget angrily as he threw the reins at the ungrateful officer. He looked back to see Birback circling his horse about as he cried out, swinging his sword about like a madman. It was a scene of complete chaos, and Hawkshaw didn't need to be told twice as he leapt back onto his horse.

"I didn't think the enemy still had such resolve," he gasped in disbelief.

"I know what desperate men can achieve, because I have been that man, and so has the Captain."

"Fall back, retreat!" Craven roared, as he assumed command. He rode to the front and held his sword high, some forming up beside him. Others fought off those still trying to press against them. Craven led them forward at a steady pace, advancing as a wall against the scattered French infantry and cavalry. A mounted French officer cried out to rally and form up, but he spoke only a few words before Moxy shot him from the saddle, having saved his rifle for just the right moment. It gave Craven just the opening he needed as the enemy were disordered.

"Charge!"

They rushed against the French troops, many of which had either lost the stomach to fight or had used up all of the energy in their starved bodies. Some fled for cover whilst others tried to put up a fight. Craven led a spearhead right through them as he hacked down one and thrust into the body of another cavalryman before breaching out into open ground. He looked back to see the others were with him but did not slow down as they heard sporadic gunfire ring out. Nobody gave pursuit, but both sides had had enough, yet Craven could see a commotion. He finally stopped and wheeled about to get a better look. Birback was still amongst the enemy, swinging wildly from one side to another until he brought down his sabre so hard onto one man's head his blade snapped at the guard. An infantryman thrust the butt of a musket towards his face, but he caught it with his left. He then hauled the man forward, smashing him in the face with what remained of his sword and tossing it at another. He took hold of the musket in both hands and swung at more of them, as though paddling a boat frantically to fight a current.

He dug his heels in as he spurred his horse on, smashing several more opponents, but he was hacked across his left arm. The musket fell from his arms as he pressed his horse on and burst out from the mass of enemy. They seemed to have let him go from the fatigue and fear of fighting such a berserker, when a musket shot rang out. It hit him from behind, and he winced in pain as he slumped over his horse. Paget drew his sword once more as if to go back.

"Hold!" Craven ordered.

Birback rose up in the saddle once more and rode on to join them. He had a smile on his face, but blood dripped from several wounds on his face as he stopped beside them. Matthys leaned in beside him for a close look. There was a hole high on the shoulder of his greatcoat, and another out the front.

"Does it hurt?"

Birback nodded back at Matthys.

"Good, you damned idiot," scolded the Sergeant.

Craven smiled as he looked back at the French village. There was no stomach for a pursuit, the streets lying littered with the dead and wounded.

"I don't need your help," Hawkshaw scowled furiously.

"Lieutenant, don't be such a fool," Matthys snapped at him, completely disregarding the man's rank in a most uncharacteristic move.

"Captain," Hawkshaw shouted back at him.

"Captain?" Paget gasped.

"He took a commission with the Portuguese." Craven smiled, now understanding why Hawkshaw rode with Portuguese light horse.

"You can get promotion in such a way, Sir?"

"It's how they get you," smiled Craven.

"This was my business, not yours." Hawkshaw stared angrily at Craven.

"I'd have left you to die if it wasn't for him." Craven unsympathetically pointed towards the Sergeant who had spoken out against him.

"Stay out of my business!" Hawkshaw then gestured to his troops and led them on.

Craven sighed in frustration.

"Why do I bother, Matthys?"

"Because you're a better man than you used to be," replied the Sergeant.

"No, because you won't bloody let me do otherwise,"

muttered Craven.

CHAPTER 2

"Well?" Wellington asked with complete exhaustion and fatigue as Craven and Paget waited before him. A fire roared in the corner so that neither him nor Major Spring needed to wear any warm clothing at all. A map in the corner of the room had gathered a layer of dust from lack of attention.

"Sir, the enemy remain at Santarem and the surrounding area," replied Craven.

"That much is clear, but what of their strength and their resolve?" Major Spring asked.

The door to the room was flung open, and Major Thornhill stormed in, tearing off a thick coat as he approached.

"I think it's fair to say the enemy's will to fight remains firmly intact," he growled.

"Wellington looked puzzled and turned back to Craven for explanation.

"You engaged with the enemy?"

"If you want information, then don't send a man who finds trouble wherever he goes."

Wellington sighed. "I'd like to think a success based on initiative could be praised, but we have not come this far based on personal initiative and a desire to fight. We have survived this damned war by the execution of orders and a great deal of planning," he complained.

"Sir, it was not my intention to seek an engagement with the enemy, and only did so in an effort to relieve our countrymen and allies."

Wellington turned to Major Spring in disbelief, but he had no answers, and it was Thorny who provided them for him.

"Captain Hawkshaw took it upon himself under his new command to head North, copying the orders of Captain Craven."

"Sir, Captain Hawkshaw and his cavalry made an assault on an enemy held village as we observed, but they were soon engaged with French cavalry. They would not have made it back had we not intervened," replied Craven defensively, but without his usual confidence and resolve.

"And you would risk your neck for this Hawkshaw? A man who so recently wanted you dead?"

"Any excuse for a scrap, Sir," smiled Craven.

"And so you did not do it out of brotherly love?" Thornhill asked.

Craven's smile quickly vanished as Wellington looked back and forth at the two of them.

"Well?" he asked Craven.

"It was as much a surprise to me, Sir, a fact not revealed until we had fought," he admitted without offering any further explanation. Wellington got up from his desk and began to pace back and forth.

"Do you know our greatest strength in this place?" he finally pondered.

"No, Sir."

"Time. We wait behind the strongest defences seen by any man who ever lived, and we are kept supplied with everything we need by sea. Time is on our side, whilst the French must maintain a vast army so far from their own lands and supply as they struggle. For keeping an army in the field for such a prolonged period of time is a logistical nightmare. An impossibility some would say. We have the army; we have the food and the powder, and all we need to wait out the enemy as they grow weaker every day that passes. Every week the Navy brings in all that we need from America, Algeria, Morocco, Ireland, Holland, and Prussia. At this time the French are not our greatest enemy. Do you know who that is?"

"No, Sir." Craven appeared lost and confused by the complexities of command.

"England. England is our greatest threat. Our politicians, our newspapers, and all who hold influence; for those who do not understand war mean to interfere with the conduct of it at every step."

"Sir, I am not sure I follow."

"You know why we are here and why we wait?"

"Yes, Sir."

"Those back home see a stalemate, and the Portuguese see the same. They hear of the woeful treatment of those left behind and of the refugees who have sought safety here behind the lines. Back home they see that the French have been stopped and no further progress made on our side. There are calls to start sending our troops back home and call an end to all this," he sighed.

"The only thing stopping the French taking all of Portugal is this army," protested Craven.

Wellington smiled. "If only there were more who saw through the same eyes and with the same mind, but you see we now turn on one another. This army and those who support it are here in this country, but back home will be the only ones who can defeat us."

"So why not attack, Sir?" Craven pleaded.

"You fought with the French this day, did you not?"

"Yes, Sir, I did."

"How did you find them?"

"They fought like starving lions," admitted Craven.

"Then you know why we do not attack. The enemy have suffered greatly over this winter, but it would be a foolish thing to think we can roll them over with such ease. No, Captain. The lines here at Torres Vedras are our strength, and I would not risk this army because short sighted politicians cannot understand the simple tactics we must maintain."

"Then what do we do, Sir?"

"We wait, and hope the fools back home do nothing brash," sighed Wellington.

Spring chuckled a little at the prospect.

"Captain, the best thing you can do right now is stay out of trouble," replied Wellington.

"Yes, Sir."

He walked away with no more insight than he had arrived with, and heard a heated discussion begin as he left. Matthys and

Paget were awaiting him, eager for more news, but they could tell from his frustrated expression that they would receive none.

"Still we sit idle?" Paget asked in frustration.

"What else were you expecting?" he scowled.

"To go at them, Sir. They are surely there for the taking."

"You think so? You saw how those Frenchmen fought. They did not run from a fight, did they? They went toward it. Imagine the fight we would have if they stood their ground and battled to the end."

"Yes, Sir, indeed a great scrap it would be," he replied enthusiastically.

"After all you have seen. How can you be so eager to step foot on the battlefield again?"

"Says the man who duels almost as often as he eats," snapped Paget.

Craven could hardly believe the cheek of the young officer, and yet Matthys chuckled in agreement, but chose to ignore it as he moved to more pressing matters.

"There is talk of us being sent back home."

"Why us, Sir?" asked Paget in annoyance.

"Not just us, the army."

"But this fight isn't over!"

"No, it damn well isn't, and if we leave now, we will only be right back here soon enough, or looking out across the channel at another invasion attempt once more," snarled Craven.

"Surely England cannot be so naive as to withdraw the army now?"

"Come on, Matthys, you know they are quite capable of that and a lot more."

"What do we do, Sir?" pleaded Paget in frustration. He and Matthys hurried to keep up with the Captain who was striding along with purpose. They passed several bodies of troops conducting drill whilst others lay about making the best of the time as they waited idle for the winter to pass, even if that meant merely walking the lines as a break from monotony. Portuguese civilians mingled amongst them, there being so little space on the fortified peninsula they now defended. They soon turned a bend into a quiet square.

"What chaos do we march towards?" Matthys asked suspiciously.

"I don't always go looking for trouble," he snapped as they turned a bend and came to a sudden halt.

"It sure has a way of finding you, though."

They found themselves facing off against Hawkshaw and a dozen of his cavalrymen. Craven's hand hovered anxiously over his sword. He peered over to Matthys; the Sergeant being surprised to see Craven was not expecting to find trouble at all.

"You just cannot help yourself, can you?" Hawkshaw roared from thirty paces.

Craven said nothing as he could not understand his brother's anguish, and yet there was even more anger in his eyes than all previous encounters.

"You could not let me have my moment of glory! This was my time!" he wailed.

"I suppose you would have preferred we left you to die back in that village?"

"We were winning a great victory and could have disengaged from the enemy when we needed. It would have been a most magnificent raid, but you had to come and make a story of it and steal it all for yourself like you always have!"

Craven was fuming now, and showing no signs of apologising, he took a few steps closer and roared in return.

"You are a reckless fool who put all of our lives in danger. You may know how to use a sword, but you know nothing of war!"

"And I suppose you do?"

"I admit I knew little when I first came to this country. I was like you. An angry brawler, but this war is a cruel but effective teacher. What you did was suicide!"

"It was my choice to make, not yours!" he screamed in return.

But Craven stormed forward towards him. Hawkshaw did not react, standing firm and expecting to intimidate those before him, but Craven showed no such respect or regard for the danger he faced. He grabbed Hawkshaw by the collar of his jacket and yanked him in close.

"It is not your choice! Everything you do has an effect on those who fight and serve beside you!"

Hawkshaw tried to resist, but he could not get himself free.

"You put us all in danger because of your own petty and childish behaviour!"

Hawkshaw finally shoved Craven hard enough to push him back two paces, but he quickly returned with a brisk punch to Hawkshaw's jaw. His head snapped aside as he stumbled a pace back. His comrades drew swords, causing Craven to do the same as he backed away a few paces. Paget ripped his sword from its scabbard and rushed to Craven's side. Matthys did the same but with no weapon in hand, holding up his arms in order to try and calm the situation.

"Gentlemen, there is no need for blood to be spilled here, not between brothers, in blood or in arms!" he pleaded.

But Hawkshaw put a finger to his mouth to find a trickle of blood. He was panting heavily in anger as his nostrils flared out, and his eyes glossed over with a murderous look of intent to do Craven serious harm. He quickly unbuckled his belt and ripped his sabre from its scabbard, throwing the belt to the ground.

"You work to keep me in your shadow in your every move, but you will no longer do so from the grave!" He came forward towards Craven.

Craven backed away as Matthys tried to come between them, but Hawkshaw smashed the ward iron of his sword into the Sergeant's face. The gilt GR cypher left a deep imprint gash in his head as he staggered back, stunned and disorientated by the blow. Paget reached out and caught him from falling.

"What are you doing?" Paget shouted in disbelief and anger as he made sure Matthys could stand on his own two feet. He leapt in between Craven and Hawkshaw, presenting the point of his sword at the man, blocking his path to the Captain.

"This is not your fight," growled Hawkshaw.

"It is as much my fight as any man's, but you would know that if you had any honour, Sir!"

Hawkshaw sighed angrily before trying to beat Paget's blade aside, but the young Lieutenant nimbly dropped his point so that Hawkshaw's found nothing but air, and once more presented it towards the Captain's chest.

"I will have satisfaction whether I must go through you or not," snarled Hawkshaw.

"Then you must go through me, Sir."

"You will not respect my right to demand satisfaction?"

"You had your chance, and the matter is now over. You can go on blaming Captain Craven for your shortcomings like a coward, or you can rise to the occasion and prove you are worthy of comparisons to him," seethed Paget.

Hawkshaw tried to press forward, thinking Paget would not act against him, only to find the point of the Lieutenant's spadroon pressed against his uniform.

"You are no killer."

"When I left England, I was not, but out here we are all killers," sighed Paget.

There was a cold sincerity in the young man's eyes, which gave Hawkshaw pause for concern. He seemed to stumble and consider his actions, and what it might mean if he were to inflict violence on the Lieutenant, a man he had no quarrel with.

"You're fighting the wrong man," insisted the stunned Matthys who was now regaining some composure, "There is no honour to be had fighting those who wear the same uniform as yourself. It is the refuge of the petty and petulant."

"What would you know about honour?" Hawkshaw looked at his Sergeant's stripes with disgust that a non-commissioned officer would talk to him in such a way, and with so little respect for his rank.

"A great deal more than you," snapped Paget who kept the tip of his sword within an inch of the Captain's chest.

But Craven pulled him aside to take his place, sword in hand but lowered by his side.

"I won't fight you, not here. There is too much at stake in this war. When the French army is broken and Napoleon is defeated, then come and find me again."

Matthys looked both surprised and impressed with his calming presence and cool headedness; particularly in light of how the exchange had begun just minutes before. Hawkshaw tried to find some words, but Craven got ahead of him.

"Stay away from me, and you won't have to worry about receiving my help, but never call into question my actions when I go to the aid of our fellow soldiers. And that Sergeant you struck. I'd have left you all for dead if it were not for him. Stay out of my way!"

Craven sheathed his sword and walked away. Paget was the most surprised of all, and he backed away cautiously with his sword held high.

"This isn't over!" Hawkshaw yelled.

"People can change, Captain, and I hope you realise that before it's too late." Paget also sheathed his sword and went on after Craven and Matthys, leaving Hawkshaw and his posse with seemingly no leg to stand on as they let them be.

"You okay?" Craven asked Matthys.

"I've been better, but also a whole lot worse," he admitted.

"He won't stop coming for you. The anger in that man runs deep," declared Paget.

"He'll stop if he is dead, and that will be sooner rather than later if he carries on like this."

"You've come a long way," smiled Matthys, which causing him to wince in pain once more.

"You think I'd kill my own brother?"

"I know you would," replied Matthys without hesitation.

"You should stay away from him, Sir. He is dangerous," insisted Paget.

"Fifty thousand Frenchmen in front of us, and you are afraid of one Englishman?"

"You may smile, Sir, but it's the punches you don't see coming that hurt the most," replied Paget as though repeating verbatim from his coach.

"He's not wrong." Matthys patted down his bloody head with a handkerchief.

* * *

Ferreira leapt back and forth, dancing about Sergeant Barros as they engaged with singlesticks. He applied all he had learned whilst helping Craven rehabilitate under the tutelage of De Rosas, and Vicenta who now observed the display with much amusement. Many of the Salford Rifles watched on, all from the warmth of their greatcoats, which were more treasured than any other item of equipment now, but the cold did not stop them from stepping outside for a little entertainment.

"You dance like a woman!" Quental yelled from the sidelines as he jokingly mocked Ferreira, who was his superior, but also one of his closest friends and would gladly mock him in a friendly manner.

Barros was quite the skilled fighter himself and came forward with attack after attack, but he fought like an experienced brawler and not a skilled swordsman. His weapon could not touch Ferreira. He struck him with ease every few exchanges with enough force to ensure he knew he had been hit, but with no malice or intent to do serious harm. Barros was getting more and more frustrated. He finally let out a loud war cry and rushed forward aggressively, forcing Ferreira to on the defence. But he did this with ease, parrying every blow until finally, he gave a brisk batter on the back of the Sergeant's blade, and it flew from his hands. The crowd cheered as his weapon bounced along the hard mud before coming to a stop.

"Good, but you have gotten sloppy!" Vicenta shouted out.

Her voice silenced them all, but more out of curiosity than anything. For they knew she could fight, but had no idea how good she really was, and seeing Ferreira's great display of skill, they were all curious to see what she could do. She took off her greatcoat, the same soldier's issue coat the rest of them wore. She handed it to Moxy, along with her sword belt as she paced over to the singlestick lying on the cold mud. Barros stepped aside. Excited cheers rang out as the crowd watched with anticipation. She slipped her boot under the stick, flicked it up into the air, and caught it. The crowd erupted into a cheer. It was just the kind of spectacle and entertainment they needed to take their minds away from the boredom and monotony of the last few months.

"I know what you know," declared Ferreira.

"You can know a thousand things, and yet never be able to piece them together in the perfect order," she smiled as she snapped into a guard position to oppose him.

"I don't hit a woman," he added.

"Don't worry, you won't," she added with sass.

Whistles and laughter echoed out from the crowd. Ferreira sighed and took up his guard, confident in his ability to win after a dominant victory over his fellow rifleman. Vicenta suddenly lurched forward, not enough for a committed attack, but enough to make him flinch, knowing how capable a fighter she was. It earned a roar of laughter from many of those watching on. He shook his head as he focused his concentration. He knew he could not hit such a skilled and capable fighter as Vicenta in an opening attack. So he lowered his guard and opened up his body as an invitation, but she did not react. He lunged forward to try another trick and feinted twice on the same side, once low and once high, before turning his blade to the other side of Vicenta's, snapping a quick cut towards her head.

The speed and precision were enough for her to show concern and parry only at the last minute, but she quickly threw a return cut with lightning-fast precision. He ducked back from it and staggered a few paces as he was off balance.

"You have come a long way," she smiled in appreciation.

"I had a good teacher."

Vicenta now came at him and laid on several cuts. None were particularly powerful, but they were enough that he had to respond to each and every one with a parry as she tested his defences. Ferreira began to smile as he thought he was getting the upper hand. He responded with a quick riposte to her face, during what he perceived was an opening, but his stick only found thin air. She nimbly voided under it and smacked him on the buttocks with her own.

Laughter rang out from the crowd as if they were witnessing some farcical stage comedy. He shot bolt upright from the blow and frowned at the humiliation, but he soon smiled and got into the spirit of things. He realised he only had himself to blame for leaving himself open, and she had done him no harm.

He got back to his guard, took a deep breath of air, and focused his concentration. He began to move his feet and dance as the Spaniards had shown him. As much as he disproved of their methods, he knew they were effective. His feet began to move in sequence with his sword arm as he circled and traversed, hopping back and forth off of either foot. Those under his command now laughed no longer, watching in amazement at how he moved with the grace of a great dancer. His training sword flashed through the air as the two opponents moved as if perfectly telegraphed. Cuts and thrusts came one after another and were parried in perfect symphony.

"You remember your training well," declared Vicenta with a smile as they continued to trade blows. Ferreira smiled back, thinking he had finally matched her blow for blow, but as he snapped a quick vertical strike towards her head, she spun out towards his right side. She slipped her blade under his knee and lifted his leg out from under him, causing him to crash down unceremoniously onto the hard ground.

Cheers rang out from the crowd. Ferreira looked embarrassed, but as Vicenta towered over him, and he gazed over to the joy in the faces of all, he could see it was what they all needed.

"I see you still have not found your fencing feet!"

All were quickly silenced. The booming tone was unmistakeable, as they looked over to see Craven had returned. A Sergeant roared out to call them all to attention, but Craven soon waved them off as if embarrassed to be treated in such a way, despite it being his right.

"What news?" Ferreira asked.

"We hold, and we wait."

Groans echoed out along the lines as reality hit home, and that the monotony they had endured would go on.

CHAPTER 3

Craven watched as Ferreira and Vicenta chatted around a large wood fire burning between their tented encampment. As like most of the army, they had to make do under canvas in bitter conditions, and yet a steady stream of wine and food kept them all in far better spirits than their adversaries. The two fighters regaled the group of tales of their great battle and many others, as though they were gladiators from ancient Rome. The crowd lapped it up with a hunger for excitement.

"The men are in good spirits," smiled Paget as he stepped up beside the Captain.

"I never would have imagined it. I thought we would surely be back in England or at the bottom of the sea by now."

"How could you have so little faith in Wellington, Sir?"

"Faith doesn't win battles, not alone. Spanish armies and cities continue to fall. The fact we remain here with our strength is remarkable. I don't believe there is a man alive who could have imagined what could have been achieved here. I doubt Napoleon will even believe it until he sees it with his own eyes."

"You think he will, Sir? You think he will come?" Paget asked excitedly.

"We better hope not. If Wellington is right, Boney is worth forty thousand troops on the field, almost as many as our entire army."

"And you think that is true, Sir?"

Craven nodded in agreement. "As I said, belief and faith cannot win fights alone, but they can tip the balance, and you know this. If it were Napoleon leading and not Masséna, he would never have stopped at the lines. He would have fought through hell to achieve victory."

"And he could have done it, in spite of all of this?" Paget gestured out North towards the lines, but they were far from in sight of them.

"As impressive as these fortifications are, Napoleon conquered the fortress that is Europe. I am not sure anything would have stopped him."

"And yet he is not done yet. For we still have this foothold, and he is nowhere to be seen."

Craven nodded in agreement at that statement.

"You truly believe that is all it would take for a French victory, for Napoleon to join the fight here?"

"He did it once before, and he was unstoppable."

"Then what is stopping him now, Sir?"

Craven shrugged.

"Then I am glad you are not advising the Emperor, or I fear we might have already lost this war."

"As I hear it, the French squabble amongst themselves as

"Look, this is important. Everything we have done here is at risk of being undermined merely because those who do not understand war feel the need to dictate how it is conducted. What we have achieved here is nothing short of a miracle. I don't think anyone would have imagined a possibility that we would still be here in Portugal going into the New Year, and yet here we are. We need to hold onto this position we have fought hard to secure. For if we lose it, then all of it will have been for nothing, and there will be no return. If Napoleon takes this peninsula, he will have it for good."

"And then on to England?"

"Why would he not? He will take the world if he is allowed to."

Craven groaned, as he knew he was going no matter whether he wanted to or not.

"All right, so what do you need?"

"I need you to take a few good men North, enough that you may deal with any small trouble, but not so many as to attract attention. I need to know what Masséna is up to, and so you will need a French speaker amongst your ranks."

"I don't have one."

"No, which is why I have secured the perfect man for the job," smiled Thorny as he pointed forwards for Craven to see the last man he would have expected to be taking along.

"You cannot be serious?" He looked upon Captain Hawkshaw, smugly standing in wait for them.

"A junior officer who can speak French as well as he fights with a sword? You could not ask for a better companion," smiled Thorny, knowing precisely how awkward he was making the situation as they stopped in front of his half-brother. The man who had wanted him dead from the moment they first met.

"Why did you come here for this?" Craven asked him.

"I only follow orders," replied Hawkshaw, as if insulted he may be there for any other reason, despite having come to Portugal to pursue his own interests.

"Listen to me, gentlemen. There will be no more fights between you. Whatever issues you have you will put aside until such time as I tell you otherwise. Is that understood? I said is that understood?"

But the two captains glared at one another as if that was never going to be a possibility, the hatred now running deep, even for Craven who until recently had no clue to his brother's existence.

Thorny placed a hand on each of their shoulders.

"Do not test me on this. This mission and this war are far more important than any quarrel you two might share. You will put it aside, or you will regret it, do you understand me?"

"For King and Country," replied Craven cynically.

"I have waited all my life to settle this score. I can wait as long as is required," replied Hawkshaw with a cold and ruthless determination.

"You see that you do. For many men have tried to end Craven, be it to his face or in the dead of night. Only a fool would know this and still pursue him, but if that is the course you must take, you will do it on your own time and not on the King's shilling. Until I say otherwise, you will watch each other's backs. That is an order."

"Yes, Sir," replied Hawkshaw.

"What do you expect us to find?" Craven asked.

"I really don't know, but I imagine it is one of three things.

He must surely be either building an army and assault force to attacks the lines, finding a way around, or digging in for when we finally push out."

"And will we, push out from behind this fortress?"

"You heard Wellington. We can't wait here forever. People back home want to see change. They want to see progress. If the enemy will not bring the fight to us, then we must take it to them."

"And then these lines will have been for nothing?"

"Not at all. They kept us alive and in this fight. Do not forget the retreat to Lisbon, Captain, not a single man gave our army a chance of halting Masséna's advance. He seemed unstoppable, and look where we are today, but that is no reason to underestimate him. Gather me the intelligence I need, and we will find a way to move forward."

Thorny then handed Craven a folded-up map.

"Here, I have added notes for everything I know of enemy positions, and our own. The Navy has troops ashore and gunboats assisting also. In that cart there are French uniforms and also Portuguese local clothing, everything you might need. Our position is strong as it stands, but that could change, for who knows what plan the enemy works toward. Good luck to the both of you, and remember, you may not like the fact you are related, but you cannot forget that you are brothers in arms. Put any foolish and selfish thoughts aside and do what must be done."

He quickly stormed away to go about his business, leaving the two captains facing each other, both with their left hands hovering over the pommels of their sheathed swords in a tense stand off.

"I'll make this work because those are my orders," declared Hawkshaw.

"Let me make myself absolutely clear. This is my mission, and I have seniority. You follow my orders. I have no desire to harm you, but if you make any attempt on my life or those of any of the Salfords, I will rightfully take yours in self-defence, do you understand?"

"I will do as it required of me."

Craven led them back to the camp where others were starting to stir, many surprised to see Hawkshaw by Craven's side.

"I won't be your second," declared Ferreira as he yawned and shook his head at the scene.

"This is not a personal matter. We have our orders," replied Craven.

"When do we move out?" Matthys asked.

"Just as soon as we are ready."

"Muster the men," Ferreira gave his order to Quental.

"Not all of us. The regiment will remain here. Ten of us are to go North."

"North? We just returned from the North, barely," protested Ferreira.

"Different day, different mission."

"And you want to take even less soldiers?"

"Not scared, are you, Charlie?" Craven smiled at her.

"Never."

"I need a few men who speak Portuguese, and I need good but subtle fighters."

"I'm in," declared Birback.

Charlie looked at him as she held back laughter.

"You don't think I can be subtle?"

"I know you can't," she snapped back.

"Nine of us and Captain Hawkshaw here it is," declared Craven.

"Eight. I shall be bringing one of my own," declared Hawkshaw as another young officer stepped up beside him.

He was an ugly and bullish looking man who had the look of one who had taken too many punches to the face, yet he had a cocky arrogance and an awkward smile. He oozed with confidence.

"This is Lieutenant William, or Bill Benning."

"Nine men, that's it, no baggage. My orders are for you to travel with us, not your friend."

"He is a fiery one," smirked Benning.

"That is Captain Craven you are speaking to!" Paget cried furiously at the lack of respect he showed.

But Benning merely spat on the floor beside himself. He was a crude and unsophisticated fellow who didn't appear to match the uniform he wore, rather as if someone had placed Craven's tunic on Birback.

The Salfords waited on Craven to make his move, but Hawkshaw got ahead of him.

"I will go with you on this mission because those are my orders, but I won't do it alone, for I won't ever make it back alive."

"You are suggesting Captain Craven would see to your untimely demise?" Paget demanded.

"It could be arranged," muttered Birback as he weighed up the two officers.

"If I am going to stab you, it will be in the front and with plenty of notice," replied Craven.

"I don't think your men share the same sentiment," replied Hawkshaw, looking at the furious expression on many of their faces.

"Nothing happens to the Captain here, or I will shoot you myself, is that clear?"

Unenthusiastic groans and nods were hardly reassuring.

"Benning comes with us. He is more than capable a fighter as any man you have," stated Hawkshaw.

Laugher echoed out from the Salfords.

"Really? Care to wager on that?"

"Sir, we cannot duel here," pleaded Paget.

"No not a duel, a friendly contest of skill," declared Craven.

"To first blood drawn from the torso with a light blade and no giving point," declared Benning.

They all knew what they meant. It was to be a bloody affair the likes of which current day gladiators were most accustomed, a fight where death and dismemberment gave way to bloodletting and pain.

"I'll take that," declared Birback with glee.

"Sergeant Gamboa, your sword!" Craven roared.

The Sergeant carried a British supplied infantry sergeant's weapon. The same form of sword Paget carried, merely with less decoration. The Portuguese sergeant didn't much like parting with it but would never question Craven's orders. Paget drew out his own treasured blade and passed it to Birback. The straight and slender single edged cut and thrust blades looked feeble in the hands of the two ruffians who looked better suited to wielding sabres fit for the cavalry.

"What are you doing?" Ferreira leaned in over Craven's shoulder as the troops spread out to form a small arena for the two gladiators.

"Only allowed to cut, and with those blades, how much damage can they do?"

But there was a cheeky grin in Craven's face, as he knew very well the narrow blades were quite capable in the right hands. They could not sever limbs, but they had all seen Paget deal with many a Frenchman with one, whether by thrust or cut.

"What are the stakes?" Matthys asked.

"Surely this is a point of honour, and victory will be reward enough," declared Hawkshaw.

"That doesn't speak to the confidence in your man," replied Craven.

"I didn't come to this country to make stupid bets and to play games."

"No, you came here to play the most dangerous game of them all," Paget added, as he looked to Craven and imagined what a mountain of a task it would be to defeat such a formidable fighter.

The two fighters stripped down to the waist as to make any cuts to their bodies clear for all to see, and to not cut their clothes to ribbons. Benning bore a number of scars, but they paled in comparison to Birback, who looked as though he had been used as target practice by the whole army. Both of their bodies were pale, as the air they breathed caused huge clouds from condensation, yet neither man would shiver in the presence of the other.

"Ready?" Craven demanded.

The two men nodded towards him before Birback came

to his guard, neither man saluting one another. Benning remained upright with his sword hanging by his side and a smug expression on his face.

"That's not a clever move," whispered Paget.

"That depends on why he's doing it. Fools and masters do the very same but for very different reasons," replied Vicenta as she watched with great curiosity.

"You think he is a skilled swordsman?"

"A confident one certainly, but it is hard to read the skill of a man who has complete confidence in himself."

"Begin!" Craven ordered.

Benning's arrogant and relaxed poise had been an act. For it was as if a wild beast had been released from its cage, as he came out swinging like a most aggressive cudgel player. Birback was surprised and yet smiled as he parried the blows and stood his ground. Yet Benning kept closing the distance as though he wanted to grapple, before smashing the ward iron of the sword into Birback's face. It cracked him in the nose and opened up a deep cut, but Birback barely seemed to notice it. He responded instinctively in kind, smashing the hilt of Paget's prized sword into his opponent's face. It split his lip open and caused him to stagger back a few paces. Birback smiled, revealing the blood in the gaps of his teeth as he seemingly asked Craven if that was enough.

"You aren't done yet," admitted Craven, remembering the simple rules they had agreed upon.

Both fighters seemed in their element, and it was now clear Benning was no stranger to violence. He revelled in it the same way Birback did. Birback closed in as Benning came to a guard position this time, his initial trick already being used. They

CHAPTER 4

The mud squelched under Craven's boots as he trudged on. The strong swirling winds caused the rain to seemingly encompass each one of them and soak everything to the core. Ferreira drove the cart on as it creaked and rattled despite the soft ground. Spirits were low, but at least there were few eyes on them as nobody would want to be out in such conditions if they could avoid it.

"Why nine?" asked Matthys as he thought of the party Craven had requested.

"We are trying to blend in, you know what a nice even number looks like?"

"A squad," admitted Matthys.

The group made slow progress as they avoided major roads and struggled on through the rain and mud, finally taking shelter amongst some trees for the night. A fire was soon a welcome relief as all of them huddled around without hesitation.

"Hardly the most glamorous work, is it?" Hawkshaw smiled.

"Because you came down to our level. You could surely have taken up a position on General staff, or perhaps even Horse Guards and played soldier at home?"

"And be the butt of every joke and constant ridicule?"

"And I suppose you think that is my fault?"

"You know it is."

"You talk like I have greatly offended you, but how could I have when I did not even know you existed?"

"Because you give us all Englishmen a bad name. Only I am the focus of so much of it because of the blood we share," snarled Hawkshaw.

"A bad name? Craven is out here getting results. This is war, and it is dirty business," snapped Ferreira who could not listen to his complaints any longer without speaking up.

"No, he fights because he enjoys it. He has no honour."

"I've known men without honour. Men who would have shot you in the back for what you have done or slit your throat without even knowing who you were. Craven would be quite within his right to run you through for what you have done."

"Then let him try, for I have not been defeated yet."

Craven sighed as the conflict between them was becoming tiresome.

"Whatever you are looking for you won't find it in fighting me," he sighed.

"I have to. It is all I have sought since as far back as I can remember. As far back as I learned of your existence and was made a mockery of because of it."

"And it's worth losing your life for?" Ferreira asked.

"I didn't come here to lose."

"Not even the most fearsome swordsman anyone has ever known was able to kill Craven no matter how hard he tried, and believe me, he tried in ways you cannot imagine," argued Ferreira.

"We have crossed blades. He is not to be feared."

"Because I didn't want to kill you," whispered Craven.

"What?" Hawkshaw demanded.

"I'll fight any man who wants it, but there is a great difference between fighting and killing."

"Am I hearing this right? That the great and daring James Craven is afraid of killing?" Hawkshaw laughed.

Benning chuckled on loudly beside him.

"What does it prove? I've killed many men, and I will likely kill many more, but I do not do it for sport."

"All I hear is excuses," replied Hawkshaw scathingly.

"Because that is all you want to hear. You are so blinded by this hatred you can't see anything else," declared Ferreira.

"And what would a Portuguese know about it?"

"What would I know about hatred? My country has been invaded for the third time by an enemy we had no quarrel with. The French have slaughtered my people and beat and starve those who remain. They turn others against each other so that brother fights brother, not over some petty jealous squabble, but for the fate of our entire country. Don't come here and talk to me about hatred! For you are a spoilt boy who cannot accept his brother has achieved greatness without any of the help you had. Craven has made something of himself and dragged himself up from nothing to this. What have you ever done? I bet you had everything, and yet here you are blaming someone else for all your problems!" Ferreira cried angrily.

Hawkshaw looked around for some sympathy, but he could see that even his one friend would not back him.

"Even you, Benning?"

"He's not wrong, but that's no reason to not take what you want," he admitted.

"And what is it that you want? Do you want me to suffer, to kill me? To humiliate me?" Craven asked.

The others were all silent now as they watched the two brothers argue.

"I want to be my own man and stop having the world judge me through a lens I have no influence over."

"Then do it. You direct your anger at the wrong person. So many people belittle you and drag you down, but not me. I am here for me and for those who stand with me. Cut your own path and stop worrying about what I do."

"That is easy for you to say when you are not the target of such ridicule," sobbed Hawkshaw as he came close to tears.

Craven looked to Matthys for help, as he so often did.

"Well? Where are your words of wisdom now?" Craven demanded.

"I am afraid it is not given where it is not wanted," replied the Sergeant.

"Bullshit, you always speak your mind whenever you care to."

"To you, yes, because I knew you long before you were an officer in this army, but it is not my place to speak to others in such a way."

"Let him hear it, and I will take responsibility for it," replied Ferreira. He was sick of hearing the dispute as the rain continued to trickle down upon them, the fire struggling to keep them warm.

Matthys could see Captain Hawkshaw was waiting for him to go on and offer some great insight. He took a deep breath before weighing in on the situation.

"You will never be rid of Craven's shadow whilst you keep chasing it. If you fall by his hand, you will just be another fool who walked to his own death. And if it is you who is triumphant, you will be disgraced for killing a great hero of this war. You will be mocked and ridiculed for it for as long as you live. Wellington will have you sent home in disgrace, and you will never stop hearing the name James Craven until the day you die."

Ferreira shook his head in disbelief, not ever expecting the Sergeant to be so brutal in his reply. Hawkshaw was stunned by it, and it was clear nobody in his life had ever dared share such a vicious truth. He looked to Benning for a second opinion.

"You believe that, too?"

"I don't bother myself with what might be. If you want to kill him, kill him, but don't expect to be treated as a hero for it. The enemy are out there, not around this fire."

"So not even you will stand by me?"

"Kill Frenchmen, and we may get promotion and medals, fame. What do we get for killing him? Probably a hundred of his angry friends coming after us, and a mob when we get home, so why bother?"

"Why bother? Do you have no principles?"

"No," replied Benning unashamedly.

Craven smiled as he could see something of himself in Benning, or at least the way he was when he first came to the Iberian Peninsula. Hawkshaw fell silent, either because he felt sheepish or because he was making no progress, but it was Ferreira who finally spoke up as he could see it was too volatile a situation to leave as it had been.

"Be angry with Craven, plenty of us are all the time, but do not stand in his way. We have enough enemies in this world already. None of us need look for more."

"And what would you do in my shoes? Sail back to England?"

"No, if you want to stop being judged because of your brother, you better make sure your name shines more brightly. Here in this great and terrible war you can do that. Craven did. Why not you? If you want to be remembered as something more than his brother, you'd better start giving people a reason to see you differently."

"And so, I just give up all that I came for?"

"Not at all. You didn't come here to kill one man. You came here to restore your reputation. You can bring glory to your name if you want it, but it will never come by targeting those who stand beside you."

Craven looked impressed.

"Is that why you are here? To bring glory to your name?"

"God no, but we must all find our way and purpose. You can find yours here if you want it."

They all fell silent in deep contemplation as they watched the roaring fire and thought of better days. They tried their best to sleep, not even caring to post anyone on guard duties, knowing nobody would be so foolish as to be out in the wilderness at night in such appalling conditions. Most fell asleep where they sat, their heads slumped down into the warmth of the fire.

Morning came quickly once their eyes were finally closed, far too quickly. The wet and cold ground gave them all cause to spring to their feet as the last warmth of the fire faded away. Not one word was spoken as they gathered their things and continued on a miserable path. The only consolation was the rain had finally stopped, but another full day's march across rough tracks and soft ground meant they would spend another night amongst the trees before the enemy positions would come into sight.

"How will we do this do you think?" Matthys asked as they sat around another fire.

"We should have donned French cavalry uniforms and ridden in and out without incident," declared Hawkshaw.

"Too big of a target, too large of a presence. We might pass as Frenchmen once or twice in the right scenario, but it is to be avoided at all costs," replied Craven.

"I wonder what good it was bringing French equipment at all," replied Ferreira.

"It could have its uses, but that damned cart will make us a mighty fine target to the French when we draw close. We shall have to keep it far from their eyes, as they will be surely eager to try and take whatever a band of locals have."

"Then we should travel as if we have nothing to take?" Hawkshaw joked.

"Precisely," replied Craven.

"Then we walk into the mouth of the lion tomorrow with nothing in our hands?"

"We have our courage and heart, Barros," replied Matthys.

"Is this the kind of work you are given?" Hawkshaw asked in amazement.

"Sometimes, there are no easy tasks in this place," admitted Craven.

"I do not need easy, but the work of a peasant brings me no joy."

"Not for them either," replied Ferreira.

The sun was soon up and bringing a little warmth to their seemingly permanently soaked clothing. As they advanced over rolling hills, they could finally see French troops in the distance.

"This will have to do. We leave everything here." Craven looked around for a good position to conceal their cart and tie the horse that pulled it.

"Nothing but what you can well conceal, small knives, nothing more." He rummaged amongst the cart and took out a knife that had clearly once been a French cavalry sword. The ward iron was missing, and the blade had been cut down and reground to just ten inches long. It was a crude looking tool but well shaped and with an excellently honed edge.

An effective little killing tool!

He pulled back his wet and dirty cloak and slipped the weapon into his belt, letting the heavy cloak fall over it to completely conceal the weapon. Hawkshaw watched in disgust before finally doing the same.

"If we are caught, we will be shot as spies."

"Then don't get caught."

Hawkshaw shook his head in amazement as they set out empty-handed and on foot with nothing more than a few concealed knives to defend themselves with.

"What do you think? Do we pass as locals?" Craven asked Ferreira.

"So long as nobody looks too closely."

"Come on. Let's press on and make the most of the day."

"We should remain close to the water. It is bitterly cold there, and we should find few Frenchmen there," added Barros.

"They would not defend the coast?" Hawkshaw asked.

"This isn't England. Neither our army nor the French control the lands. They maintain control wherever their armies go and a few miles around, but no more," replied Craven.

"Why?" Hawkshaw could not imagine such a possibility after his upbringing in England.

"Because my people don't want them here, and they will murder the French at the first opportunity, and so they can only travel in large numbers. They cannot control all the land, only small pockets," replied Ferreira.

Craven went forward a few paces and stopped in the open for all to see for some distance, no longer fearing being spotted by the enemy, as they were seemingly a few peasants with nothing worth taking. The wind still battered them and caused their cloaks to flutter about, lashing them as they tried to hold them down. Far into the distance they could see French positions, thousands of troops in cantonment just as they were behind the lines, with tens of thousands more far from view. It seemed an insurmountable task for the small group.

"Is this how Captain Craven made a name for himself? Out here on the frontier with little but a few blades and the odds stacked against him?"

"I made a name for myself the same way I always have. I fight, and I win."

"Except we aren't here to fight. They sent a swordsman to do a spy's work," replied Ferreira.

"So, how do you propose we do this?" Hawkshaw asked.

"We are here to gather intelligence. We advance and learn what we can whilst avoiding a fight. If we are approached, only Ferreira and Barros speak. We are peasants who want nothing to do with the French. Do not make eye contact with them, and do not show any strength nor resilience, for they will soon want to beat it out of you."

"And if we are beaten?"

"Then you will take it. For nothing short of the risk of death can be excuse enough to fight back. To do so could risk all of our lives."

Craven led the way forward with Ferreira by his side.

"This is a terrible idea. You understand that, don't you?" he whispered.

"Come up with a better one, and I am all ears," replied Craven.

They marched on in as staggered and ill formed a manner as they possibly could to try and blend in. It was not long before they could see French pickets at the edge of one village.

"What do you want to do?" Ferreira asked.

"We pass right on through. We are looking for work to fill our bellies, that is all."

"And if they offer us work?"

"They have fifty thousand idle soldiers to put to work, why would they?"

"You think they will let us just walk on past?"

"So long as they think we have nothing worth taking, yes."

Ferreira groaned as they anxiously ambled towards the Frenchmen who looked down upon them with disgust. They heard the gallop of horses as a troop of cavalry scouts roared past. They knew if they were found out there would be no chance of escape, and so they went on hoping for the best. One of the Frenchmen yelled some insults in Portuguese which Craven did not understand the meaning, but he knew their intention as he had heard them before.

Ferreira hissed quietly as if ready to boil over. Craven merely touched his flank as if to threaten to stab or punch him there, as a reminder to hold his tongue. The same Frenchman came forward and yelled out in French before shoving Joze. He staggered a few paces before going on without issue, for he was accustomed to such behaviour long before the French arrived. He was the sort to take the abuse in public before returning with a knife in the night to take his revenge. But the Frenchman then shoved Hawkshaw who lost his footing and tumbled into a slick of wet mud. He looked furious, but Craven quickly appeared beside him, offering out his hand to help him up. Not for any love of the man, but for a desire to survive the experience. He was hauled to his feet, only for them to see an officer approaching and posing questions in broken Portuguese.

"He asks what we are doing here," whispered Barros as Ferreira addressed the new problem.

Ferreira was quick to respond in a flurry of words, playing the role of an exasperated and desperate man well. Finally, the weary looking officer gave up and yelled for them to go on. Ferreira looked back with a smile as he led them forward. They went on through the village where some of the soldiers looked down upon them with disdain, but most were too exhausted or weak from hunger to be bothered. They soon reached the far side of the village when a voice cried out in French, and Hawkshaw instinctively responded. Craven felt his stomach turn, knowing the game was up. He turned back to see the officer who had hassled them had come for a second look.

"He thinks we are French deserters," said Ferreira as he understood far more of the language than the others.

Craven looked around. They were in a quiet area between two small houses. He ambled slowly towards the officer, holding up his left hand as if to argue with him, but as he approached, he smothered the officer's mouth with his left hand. He drew out his cut down sword and drove it into the man's body. His eyes opened wide in horror, but he barely made a sound as Craven's hand was held firmly over his mouth. He lowered him down to the ground as he faded away and drew out the blade.

Hawkshaw looked on in horror, imagining that it could have been him had their positions been reversed. But Benning was entertained by the brutal display. Yet Craven was already looking around like a hawk for any other sign of trouble. Nobody had seen what he had done. He sheathed his blade and lifted the dead officer by his shoulders, hauling him towards a door to one of the houses.

"Clear that up," he ordered, pointing to a pool of blood.

Moxy was quick to drag his boot over the pool and mixed it with mud until it was indistinguishable. Craven backed through the doorway and stopped briefly. To his relief the small house was empty and clearly made up for another officer to live out a relatively comfortable winter.

"It won't take them long to find him," insisted Matthys as he imagined how precarious their situation now was.

"What do we do?" Hawkshaw asked.

"Make it look like it was one of their own," insisted Ferreira.

"What?"

"You have seen them. The French are tired, angry, starving, and sick. I am willing to bet many a man would be willing to kill for a little food, a blanket, or some trinkets he may trade for the same."

Craven drew out the dead officer's sword and turned him over, plunging the sword into the wound he had created. He then lay the sword down on the ground.

"This is barbaric," declared Hawkshaw.

"This is war, not a game of cards."

"Take anything of value, and do not leave any food, wine, or water," Ferreira added.

Matthys and Joze quickly gathered up anything they could from the small house. Craven took the officer's whistle and a small bag of coins he had on him.

"The poor fellow was only doing his duty."

"Yes, and let us not meet the same fate," insisted Craven.

He was soon happy with the scene they had set as he rushed to the door to find the others keeping watch.

"We have to leave, now!"

They walked out casually and towards a line of trees, looking back occasionally and acting as calmly as possible.

"Do you think whoever discovers that man will believe the story you have left for them to find?" Hawkshaw asked glumly.

"We hope to be so lucky, but plenty of soldiers saw us move through that camp. They could just as easily assume it was us."

"And we have to presume they will," added Matthys.

"Any ideas?" Craven asked Ferreira.

"We move by land. If they come after us it will be by horse."

"Okay?" Craven asked, as if expecting an answer, not a statement of the obvious.

"Then we go by water," added Ferreira.

"Is that wise?" Hawkshaw asked.

"It's better than the alternative."

"Which is what?"

"That we are run down by French cavalry. I do not fancy our odds against horsemen armed with nothing but a few daggers. Ferreira, lead the way."

CHAPTER 5

The sun was just coming up. Their small fishing boat was known as a Toldo, a flat bottom vessel that floated low in the water. It looked like a large version of the Venetian gondola, but a thin and rough mast stretched up to the sky with a single spritsail, which trapped only a little wind as the conditions had calmed somewhat. Barros and Moxy were at the bow crossing their oars, rowing from a standing position on the opposite side from where they were standing. They occasionally used their large heavy bladed oars to assist in directing the vessel's direction. Meanwhile, Ferreira was standing on a raised aft platform, acting as the helmsman with both hands on a long rudder. Craven was beside him, Captain Hawkshaw and Benning, too. The other men hid in the middle of the boat under the shelter of an old canvas canopy where fish would be stored or wine carried.

They were one of many boats out on the Tagus River, which was two to three hundred yards wide where they were. It stretched Northeast through Portugal before stretching far to the East through Spain, being the longest river in the entire Iberian Peninsula, and as a result so often of such important strategic value. Among the other boats they fit in perfectly as Ferreira greeted the passers-by in a way that would not raise suspicions, for having come from a city of fishermen he knew their mannerisms well.

"Do you have to speak with them?" Hawkshaw muttered.

"We must assume the French have spies amongst them, or informants at least," whispered Ferreira.

"The people of this country might hate the French for the most part, but we have encountered those who do not, and who fight against their own people," said Craven.

"That, and desperate people will offer up a lot for what they need to survive," replied Ferreira.

They watched a party of French cavalry carefully as they watered their horses at the riverbank but continued on unnoticed by the enemy as they mingled amongst other boats. They drew no more than a cursory glance from anyone who might bring them trouble.

"What are we even looking for?" Hawkshaw asked Craven.

"I don't know, something."

"How can we know we have found what we are looking for when we don't know what it is?"

"Look at that, what do you see?"

Craven was looking out to the far bank. Dozens of men were at work felling trees with axes. Some were soldiers whilst others were locals likely pressed into service without pay.

"The army must need a great deal of firewood to get

through this winter."

Craven dropped down and lay in the boat. He pulled out his spyglass and rested it on the edge, pulling his cloak up and over to conceal it from prying eyes. Hawkshaw knelt down beside him.

"It's the same for us. We send parties out to gather wood," he insisted.

"To be taken to the towns and cantonments, yes?"

"Yes, anywhere our troops are placed."

"But not these."

Hawkshaw looked puzzled as he lay down beside Craven and took the spyglass from him. He first looked to the wood where the timber was being collected before following the carts taking it away. He did not have to follow them far, as just a few hundred yards down a spur in the river he found many men at work with the wood, cutting and shaping it. At first glance it appeared nothing out of the ordinary.

"What are they doing? Why put so much labour into firewood?"

"They aren't making firewood."

Hawkshaw looked more closely and followed more of the work party where he could see others hammering and joining planks.

"They're building boats!" Hawkshaw gasped.

"Yes, and a lot of them."

"To do what, sail around our lines and attack Lisbon?"

"Or avoid it altogether. If they could establish a pontoon bridge here, Masséna could have his entire army across and heading South. He could ensure the rest of the country falls and join up with the French army in Spain. Badajoz would fall in days."

"A pontoon bridge, to cover this river? They would need hundreds of boats."

Craven nodded in agreement as Hawkshaw looked more closely. He could see many dozens stacked in readiness.

"We must get this news to Wellington. If the French armies are allowed to join forces, we will never see them out of this country," declared Hawkshaw in an exasperated manner.

"Calmly now. We are just fishermen going about our day." Craven took the spyglass back and took one last look for himself. He then turned back to Ferreira with a smile, knowing their work was done.

"Bring us about. I think it's time we were on our way."

Ferreira quickly obliged, as they were all relieved to be heading away from the tremendous danger they had been forced into. It was a great weight that had been lifted, and to be returning with such vital news made it all the sweeter.

"What now?" Hawkshaw asked.

"We ride the river back to Wellington, and we are done with this."

Sighs of relief echoed out. As they passed from the view of the enemy, they lay down and began to contemplate how bad the situation could have been, and how closely they had come to capture and death. Yet they had not been travelling for long when Ferreira spoke out in a concerned tone.

"Look." He pointed out to a scout troop of French cavalry galloping about the countryside on the West bank.

"They are no concern of us now," replied Craven.

"They will when they find that cart."

"How?" Craven replied as he tried to shrug off what he

was saying.

"If they have found the body of that officer, and now find a cart full of uniforms and equipment, enough for nine men, the same number of peasants many of them saw pass through that village, it won't take long for them to put the pieces together," replied Matthys.

"They'll think we are nothing but deserters."

"Except we came from the British lines. They will suspect it, and that may be enough for them to believe we are in fact who we really are."

"How would that matter now?" Craven asked.

"Because we return to Wellington with news of what is happening here, but if the enemy suspect we know of their plans, they might change them altogether, and this was all for nothing. It could jeopardise everything," replied Matthys.

Craven growled in frustration as he'd imagined them sailing back home, resting his feet in relative comfort.

"That is a lot of assumptions to make," he sighed as he tried to find some way to ignore it.

"And the horse? What deserter would leave the horse? He'd ride it or eat it," added Moxy as he piled on the pressure.

Craven's head dropped into his hands as he sighed again, knowing what they must do.

"Bring us ashore, then."

"We aren't going to get away without a fight."

Craven nodded in agreement with Hawkshaw who was looking out at the body of fifteen cavalrymen.

"And how do you propose fighting cavalry with nothing but a few short blades?"

Craven looked about when his focus tightened on the

large and heavy bladed oars Barros and Moxy were using to help direct them to the shore. There were another two like them inside the boat.

"No, you cannot be thinking it?"

"We use the tools we have to hand."

"You can't fight war with a few old oars," protested Hawkshaw.

"Is a great swordsman only great with the sword?"

"Why would he need to be anything else?"

"You have your answer," he replied, looking out towards the cavalrymen.

"They might never find what we left behind," replied Joze in hope that the seemingly suicidal contest could be avoided.

"Heavy cart tracks in a land where there is no food nor wine to transport? They will find it," admitted Craven.

Ferreira directed the boat towards a shallow part of the river edge and beached the bow of the flat-bottomed boat, causing them to slide up onto the soft mud. They leapt out and hauled the vessel further ashore.

"Do we not risk leaving this evidence, too?"

"No one will question an old fishing vessel," Craven answered Hawkshaw, as he took out one of the giant oars. He held it in two hands as he got a feel for the handling. It was a cumbersome instrument, but it had the one thing they were lacking, range. Barros and Moxy held onto theirs, for he had no rifle or musket with which to use the best of his skills, whilst Matthys picked up the last of them.

"So how do we do this?"

"We head for the cart. If we can make it before they do, we will have weapons at our disposal," replied Craven.

"And if we don't?"

"We make do with what we have." Craven started forward with a new sense of focus.

"It's a strange day when you wish Birback was here to help," smiled Moxy towards Matthys, as he looked at the huge oar which was rather better suited to the ruffian, they all knew Birback was. A fact he always relished.

"We still have surprise on our side. We look like a few locals going about our business," replied Matthys as they followed on after Craven.

Their feet were well rested now, and a small trek was most welcome after having frozen aboard the fishing boat. Except for Moxy and Barros who had put their back in all the way, so much so that Craven was soon moving at a jog as he carried the oar up the trail. He moved with such speed and determination the others struggled to keep up, despite most of them not having anything to weigh them down like he did. He came up over a ridge. The French cavalry had gathered as two of them pulled away foliage, uncovering the cart they had hidden amongst trees and the horse that was still tied there.

"It's time we made ourselves known," declared Craven.

"As what?" Ferreira asked.

"We are fishermen, having to keep our things secret so they are not stolen by others."

"Monsieur! Monsieur!" Craven cried as he approached them.

"This is crazy," muttered Hawkshaw.

"Yes, and it's the most fun we've had since we came to this damned country," replied Benning.

The Frenchmen turned to face them with a puzzled and

amused expression as Craven came to a halt ten yards short of them. They arrogantly showed no concern for Craven and his party at all, sitting high in their horses as they lorded it above those they perceived as filthy peasants. Craven nodded towards Hawkshaw for him to go on, being the fluent French speaker amongst them.

He stuttered and hesitated for a moment before suddenly bursting out into almost song, as the French language flowed from his tongue most enthusiastically and naturally. Ferreira leaned in over Craven's shoulder, translating as best he could. The officer leading the body of cavalry smiled in a most amused fashion, as he led his horse forward a few paces to take up a commanding position before his troops. He studied each of them closely and carefully before finally speaking, but to their amazement he did not reply in French, but in English.

"You are no Portuguese, nor a Frenchman. The arrogance of English spies knows no bounds," he smiled as his hand reached for his sabre, but Craven sprang into action.

He leapt forward and brought the head of the giant oar down to the French officer's level and thrust forward. It smashed the blade into his throat, crushing his windpipe as he was launched out of his saddle. He took another few paces as the other Frenchmen fumbled to draw their sabres in a panic. Craven had smashed one of them over the head before the first weapon had even left its sheath. He took the oar across his body and tossed it at two others. The horse of one was struck in the face and reared up, throwing its rider. It crashed into the other, causing it to bolt, and throwing its rider also.

Craven rushed to the officer he had hit to find he was gurgling as he suffocated. He grabbed the Frenchman's sabre and ripped it from its scabbard, just as he heard the hammering of a horse's hooves approach. He looked up just in time to see a cavalryman ride up to strike him with his sabre primed above his head. Before the blade could descend, a massive blow from an oar struck him from Moxy. It snapped in half as the man fell from his mount, and Moxy drove the splintered oar into his body.

Craven leapt onto the horse of the officer he had downed at the very beginning and wheeled about to join the fight as one galloped towards Barros. But the Sergeant dropped the base of the oar to the ground and buttressed it against his back foot, lowering the tip of the oar down to use it like the long pike of old. The cavalryman run onto the head of the oar and was launched from his horse. Whilst the man was still stunned on the ground, Benning pounced on him and drove a knife into his neck and liberated him of his sabre. The rest of the cavalrymen had recovered from the shock of the violent attack and were now swarming about them.

Moxy reached into the holster saddle of a riderless horse and took out a pistol. He cocked the lock and took careful aim as a Frenchman came at him, but he pulled the trigger to find it snapped and did not fire.

"French shit!" he cried, tossing the pistol at his attacker, but it was parried away with the cut of the man's sabre. He kept coming for Moxy. He ducked under the first blow and nimbly leapt off to one side, but the horseman wheeled about to make another pass at him. He had only covered half the distance before a swing of Matthys' oar sent him tumbling out of the saddle. The Sergeant tossed the lump of wood to Moxy before grabbing hold of the felled man. He picked up the sabre he had dropped and thrust it into its owner without mercy or a second thought, despite his resistance to bloodshed in so many scenarios. He leapt onto the horse of his vanquished foe and formed up beside Craven just as he ran his sabre through another.

Joze was cut across the crown of his head but smiled as he held his bloody knife high. He called for another opponent, and Hawkshaw took a horse and rode up to join Craven and Matthys. The three horsemen faced off against the remaining eight Frenchmen. A shot rang out, and one of them fell from his horse. They all looked about to see the barrel of a smoking musket in the hands of Moxy. He was standing on the top of the cart the Frenchmen had only just discovered. But seeing he had fired his shot, they paid him no more heed, and a sergeant cried out to encourage his men. Yet as he did so, he was shot through by another musket shot. The others looked back to see Moxy throw away another musket before taking up another from the stash at his feet.

The remaining cavalry quickly wheeled about as they turned to face him, but he had shot another dead before they had even closed any distance. Once again, he tossed away a musket and drew out another. Craven dug his heels in, and the three Englishmen galloped on to cut off the cavalrymen, watching in amazement as Moxy shot one after another from their saddles, being an easy target as they approached straight towards him.

When the French cavalrymen finally reached him, there were only two still in their saddles. He reversed the musket he had in hand to handle it by the smoking muzzle from an elevated position of the cart so they could not run him down. He swung the musket about like a giant club, beating away their sabre blades before Craven finally ran one through and Hawkshaw engaged with the other. They parried several blows back and forth. Hawkshaw clearly found the heavy sabre to lack the agility of his favoured blade. Yet he soon found his opening, using the mass of the blade to smash down against his smaller opponent. It cleaved into his neck and fell him in one.

Moxy had a huge smile about him as he looked at his handy work. He had done the job of an entire squad with the hoard of loaded muskets he had sat on. They looked back to see Joze and Benning finishing the survivors off with their knives with no mercy shown. Not even Matthys protested, knowing the importance of their mission being kept a secret. Craven spotted Ferreira standing casually with a knife in his hand, having done no work at all, and feeling quite proud of the fact.

"You don't think you could have helped!" Craven yelled.

"You were doing such a fine job I did not want to get in your way," he smiled.

"What do you want to do with the bodies?" Hawkshaw asked.

"Leave them," replied Craven.

"And when the enemy find them?"

"They will assume they were killed by Bandidos or guerrillas, and those men will welcome the fame and reputation it will earn them."

Benning was positively beaming as he approached them with blood on both hands. He appeared as a wealthier and more unhinged version of Birback, yet also more intelligent.

"Now that is why I came here," he rejoiced.

"You came here because I asked you," replied Hawkshaw.

"That is why I didn't give it a moment's thought. I should have come sooner."

Craven looked impressed with the way they had all handled themselves, but his expression turned to scorn as he looked upon Hawkshaw.

"Don't ever try and impersonate a Frenchman ever again!"

"It always works back home. The ladies are quite fond of it."

"Have you ever heard a Frenchman convincingly pretend to be English?"

Hawkshaw hesitated for a moment before shaking his head.

"Next time think before you talk. A Portuguese peasant speaking in broken French might make headway with the enemy and convince them of many things, but a well-spoken Englishman will never be seen as anything else."

Hawkshaw looked sheepish as he reflected on it, nodding in agreement as Craven turned away.

"Craven?" It caused him to turn back, "I know how to fight, but I don't know how to soldier, nor to spy or really much else. I can make polite conversation in London, and I can fight with the best, but I never claimed to be anything more."

"Stay alive long enough, and you will learn, or you will die."

"Will you help me?"

Craven paused and looked at him in disgust before turning to Matthys, already knowing what he would find. He sighed, as he knew he would be pressured into it, and Hawkshaw's genuine expression made it all worse.

"I don't carry dead weight, and I don't like people who try

to kill me, is that clear?"

Hawkshaw sighed in disappointment.

"It is a hard life in this army, and I need people I know can handle a sword and won't stick it in my back. If you can be that, then perhaps we can be more than we are."

"Thank you, Captain, it means a lot."

"Take the weapons, leave the horses, and let's get moving!" Craven roared.

CHAPTER 6

Wellington deliberated over a map as he and Major Spring talked quietly. Craven and Hawkshaw quietly waited in front of his desk. A roaring fire on one side of the room was a welcome relief, giving the lavish house a homely feeling to the two men. They had only slipped into their dry uniforms moments before and were still cold to the bone. Wellington finally sat back in his chair and sighed as he looked at the two of them.

"A pontoon bridge? Do you know what this will mean?"

"Yes, Sir," replied Craven.

"I am not sure that you do truly understand the full extent of how this could change the war. The pressure is on for us to crush Masséna's army, and we may yet do it if given a little more time. But if he can cross over the Tagus, then all of Portugal and Spain will be gone to the French. We cannot defeat a combined French army, and we cannot stay here forever on this small patch of rock."

"The war will be over because of one bridge, Sir?" Hawkshaw asked.

"It could well be, and the time is not yet right for an advance beyond these lines."

"Sir, send in the Navy. They have gunboats ready to use," insisted Hawkshaw.

"This is not the open seas, and any boats which travel too far up the Tagus will be met by cannon and even musket fire. The results of which will be devastating," replied Major Spring.

"No, we will need a far more delicate solution to this problem. We must keep Masséna on this side of the river just a little longer so that we may attack him directly."

"What can we do?"

Wellington gave Craven a puzzled expression, astonished he was volunteering, and yet he looked to the other man and remembered they were brothers. He smiled, for he could see the competitiveness between them had already begun.

"Brute force is not always the answer. We are not going to destroy those boats. We are going to have the French do it for us," smiled Wellington.

"Sir?" Craven asked in amazement.

"Colonel Gramont!" Major Spring yelled.

An unmistakable Frenchman strolled into the room, holding himself with an aristocratic air and the finest cut of cloth from the end of the seventeen hundreds. He was in his mid-forties at least but looked spry and healthy. He snapped to attention as though he were in uniform.

"Colonel Gramont here is a loyalist who opposes the revolution and Napoleon and would see France returned to greatness once more."

"Greatness? Has Napoleon not conquered half of the world like Alexander the Great?" Craven asked cynically.

"The great powers should not war with one another, not like this," insisted Gramont.

"The Royalists would have the French Monarchy restored, and with it a return of captured lands and the borders made what they should be," insisted Wellington.

"What has any of this got to do with the boats and that pontoon bridge?"

"The French communication lines are in tatters, as you know. Masséna sent five hundred troops to deliver a message to France, that is the extent at which we have troubled French supply and communications."

"I think we rather had some help," declared Craven.

"Yes, guerrillas and bandits harass the French everywhere they go, but now we need a more delicate touch."

Craven chuckled at the prospect as he was far from such a thing.

"Colonel Gramont here has twenty men at his disposal, and I would have him deliver a message which would see those boats go up in flames," declared Wellington.

"If you want a message delivered, let me do it."

"You have some tremendous skills, Captain Craven, but you are not capable of convincing anyone you are a French messenger."

Hawkshaw nodded in agreement as they were both reminded of the last time they had spoken French to French soldiers, and instantly been recognised as anything but French.

"I don't think I am going to like this plan," muttered Craven.

Wellington got to his feet, took a pace stick, and pointed along the coastline to the North.

"The Navy will deliver Colonel Gramont and fifty of your men here, where you will be thoroughly outfitted in French uniforms. Colonel Gramont will travel under significant escort to deliver orders which will achieve what we need."

"Seventy horsemen? We will be large target," protested Craven.

"Yes, and you will be the target of every Portuguese bandito and guerrilla along the way. And don't expect anything but hostility from any local populace who remained in their homes. French messengers must travel with such protection in these days, or they never make it to their destination. You must arrive at Masséna's line with such a significant force nobody would question it."

Craven sighed as it sounded like an awful plan, and yet he could understand the merits of it.

"May I volunteer my services for this mission, Sir?" Hawkshaw asked.

"Volunteer? These are your orders also," snapped Wellington.

"Sir, I…" began Craven.

"Damn it, Captain, I know you have history with this man, but he is a capable fighter and has a grasp of the French language. He will be invaluable to your work."

Craven sighed before accepting his fate.

"When do we leave, Sir?"

"First thing in the morning, so get a good night's rest. By your estimates, Masséna could have that bridge built in two or three weeks, and it cannot be allowed to happen. You will see to the destruction of those boats by any means necessary, do you understand?"

"Yes, Sir." Craven saluted and left with Hawkshaw in tow.

"Do you think it can be done?" he asked once they were out of the room.

"Maybe, but if we want to live beyond the next two weeks, we better be sure we find a way."

"And yet you did not want me on this mission?"

"Why would I? I can't trust you, and now we set out on a mission far more dangerous than the last. You almost got us all killed last time."

"Me?"

Craven stopped and placed an angry finger on Hawkshaw's tunic.

"You have skills and talents, that much is true, but you have no idea how to use them in the right time and place, and that makes you a danger to us all."

A deliberate and loud cough echoed out beside them, causing them to turn and face Colonel Gramont. He had been listening in.

"What?" Craven was less than impressed to be interrupted by a snobbish Frenchman, but Gramont made no apologies as he went on.

"This discontentment between two officers will not do, not where we are going. We must fit in with a French army, or it will cost all our lives."

Craven looked furious and Hawkshaw, too.

"Your job is to get us through French lines and convincingly deliver a message. Mine is to keep us alive getting there and hopefully back out. You worry about your job, and I'll worry about mine," snarled Craven.

"We depart at noon aboard the Sampson. I shall have horses, uniforms, weapons, and all accoutrements required for you and your men. You merely need to bring your bodies."

"No time to be fitted and become accustomed with this equipment?" demanded Craven in amazement, who had spent endless hours practicing with the tools he used, and the equipment associated to them.

"We must assume Napoleon has spies everywhere, the same as the English. We will do nothing to raise suspicions." Gramont turned and left without waiting for a response.

"He is right I suppose."

"Why do you come with me? Why must you keep following me?"

"I am only doing my duty. You showed me why I should pursue more than this feud we have, and now you scold me for doing so?"

"There is no feud between us. I never knew you existed, and I never wanted to fight with you. That is your problem to get over. Why, oh why, can you not just leave me in peace?"

"We may not be brothers in your eyes or mine, and we may never be, but we are brothers in arms, and that much cannot be denied. You need men who can fight. I am here, and I bring good fighters with me. Use us, Captain, use us for what we were born for."

Craven took a deep breath, knowing he would not be rid of his newly discovered brother.

"You know I think you were less hassle when you wanted to kill me?"

"Then perhaps I have found a better way, death by a

thousand cuts," replied Hawkshaw with a straight face.

"All right, it's not like I have a say in the matter either way. Come with us. Ride into the French camp playing Frenchmen, but never try and converse with them again. I don't even speak French, and I would have known what you were the moment you opened your mouth, understood?"

"I don't intend to make the same mistake twice."

Craven laughed. "None of us do, and yet still it keeps on happening," he replied before they parted ways.

Hawkshaw smiled as for anyone listening in it would appear they hated one another to the core. Yet compared to his past encounters, he could not help but feel relieved.

Craven got back to camp to find the Salfords gathered around several fires before the sun had gone down. For that was life in the winter. So few Portuguese homes even had fireplaces, and so one had to either sit at a fire outdoors or wrap up and endure the bitter cold under shelter.

"Sir, I hear by all accounts the mission could not have been more of a success," announced Paget.

"Yes," he sighed.

"What is it, Sir?" Paget was concern as he could see the worry in Craven's eyes.

"How is your French, Lieutenant?"

"Passable, Sir."

"Then tomorrow you will be joining us. Almost fifty of the Salfords."

"Where are we going, Sir?"

"Right now, I cannot say, but you will know soon enough."

Paget was anxious to know, but he knew the importance

of keeping the secrets of an army and so pressed no further.

"If you cannot tell me anymore about what you learned and where we must go, can you at least tell me if you believe we still have a chance of victory here?"

Craven shrugged.

"Honestly? It hangs in the balance for so many reasons, but if we can do what is required of us, and keep on doing that, then I think there is hope."

"Who will you take?" Matthys leaned in beside Craven.

"The best of us, because if we fail, we will have to fight like the most savage and wild beasts to ever make it back."

"I am one of the best of us?" Paget smiled.

"You always were," replied Craven honestly,

"And if you fail, what will the rest of the regiment do, having lost forty of its best?"

"If we fail, Matthys, I am not sure it will matter," admitted Craven, giving some hint as to how much hung in the balance and was being placed on their shoulders.

"Lord Wellington must have some faith in us to lay so much responsibility upon us," declared Paget.

"Perhaps, then again we may be his only choice. Where we go tomorrow is not soldiers' work," declared Craven mysteriously. He fell silent and watched the lick of the flames as they helped him forget the bitterness they had endured.

* * *

Craven watched Gramont and Hawkshaw's men boarding the Sampson. Many of the Salfords had gathered to see the forty men leave, not knowing their destination nor potential fate, only

"Yes, two days, I should imagine."

"And we can pass for Frenchmen? It did not go so well last time."

"Which is why we have Colonel Gramont and his loyalists. Who better to pass as French soldiers than…French soldiers?"

"And you trust them, Sir?" Paget asked.

"No, I do not, but we have our orders."

"A Colonel? He is in charge, then?" Matthys asked.

"No, he is no Colonel in this army. This operation is ours. Gramont and his men are nothing more than actors playing their part."

"And if it comes to a fight? Can they also fight, Sir?" Paget asked with concern.

"If it comes to a fight then we have likely already lost, but so long as everyone keeps their mouths shut and focuses on the task at hand, we might just make it."

"Sir, why send the best swordsmen in the army to conduct a mission where swords cannot win the day?"

"Because the sword is not the real weapon, but the man behind it," smiled Craven.

"It takes bravery or stupidity to walk into the headquarters of a French army fifty thousand strong or more," admitted Matthys.

"Yes, it does," nodded Craven.

"And we have all that we need to make this trick work?"

"According to the Colonel, we do."

"I don't like this, Sir, I do not like it one bit."

"And Hawkshaw, you brought him and his men also?" Matthys asked with curiosity.

"A number of them speak French, and we know they can

certainly fight." Craven looked across the deck to see his brother and Benning's murderous eyes glaring back at him.

"And do you trust them?" Paget asked.

"Maybe I shouldn't, but yes, I do. Hawkshaw came here looking for something the same as I did, and neither of us found it, but we both found something else. More than anything he wants purpose, and he will find that in victory, not in the duel."

Matthys looked at him in disbelief and amazement.

"What? What's wrong?"

"The Craven I knew solved every problem with the blade, or at least he tried to."

"And it is still the best tool available, but I'll admit it isn't always the right one," he grinned.

* * *

Craven heaved on an oar as they rowed to the coast. The boats were filled with not just troops but many sacks of equipment, and a skeleton crew of sailors, barely enough to sail the boats back to the ship. They moved towards an isolated bay that would have made a fine fishermen's wharf were it not so far from any towns and roads. The land was untouched by the war and quite beautiful, despite the stark winter conditions. They soon got ashore and pulled the boats up onto the beach, as the horses clambered out from the freezing water. Craven sighed as he looked around at the party. It was a respectable body of well-equipped troops, but also a mix of his closest friends, those who had been his enemy, and others who he had yet to fully know where they stood.

They moved inland and carried their supplies to a natural

shelter amongst some trees. Craven finally stopped them, far from view of even the Royal Navy sailors; such was the secrecy of their operation. They all knew what they had to do as they pried open the sacks and began to pull out heaps of French uniforms and equipment, which they swapped for their own. They were soon dressed in fine hussar uniforms, some captured, and others tailored in Portugal to match them; a great undertaking which spoke to the value of their mission and the thought and preparation that was the foundation of it. They wore pale blue breeches, tall leather boots reaching their knees, and red jackets. To which Craven could only smile at, for no British hussar would be seen in red, but he was reminded of the Volunteer cavalry back home who perpetually drilled and showed off to the locals in their finery. Though it also brought back memories of Ireland, a conflict he had long tried to forget, and yet now seemed completely overshadowed by the vast scale of the war in Portugal and Spain. He placed a busby over his head and now looked like all those around him. For he was dressed as a trooper, as the French Royalists played the part of their officers.

"One of us now?" Birback joked.

It did not sit well with Craven at all to see Colonel Gramont in all his finery, and his troops seemingly taking charge. The Frenchmen came through them, adjusting their equipment and giving advice to how it should be worn. Gramont himself adjusted Craven's equipment.

"This is still my command, no matter what jacket I wear, understand?"

"Yes, but we are all stage performers now, Captain, and this is theatre. The enemy have spies everywhere, and so do the guerrillas. Those dressed as officers must act as them."

Craven groaned in frustration.

"You do not trust me?"

"Why would I?"

"No reason yet, but you should know my hatred of Napoleon runs even deeper than yours. You see how these Portuguese and Spanish fight to have their country back? As I do the same for France. And I will be treated as a traitor and a spy the same as you if we are captured."

"If you are who you say you are," snarled Craven.

"You believe I would conduct this elaborate a plan to trap fifty Englishmen?"

"Bouchard would."

"I have heard of this Bouchard, and I also heard something most curious."

"Yes?"

"I heard Captain Craven had the chance to kill that man. The man who had caused him so much suffering and loss, and yet he spared him."

"And if I did?"

"Men like Bouchard are snakes. You do not reason with them, nor show them any mercy. The next time you have a chance to kill that man, I advise that you do not hesitate."

"And you, would do the same to Napoleon?"

"In a heartbeat. For some men are too dangerous to let live."

"Even if that meant killing a helpless man?"

"I would smother Napoleon in his sleep with his own pillow if I ever had such a chance."

Craven chuckled and was glad to see they had some

common ground, and yet he could not shake his suspicions.

"From now on, I must be seen to lead these men. I know what must be done, Captain. I know where to go and I know how to act. You are only here to provide the best chance of survival should the worst happen."

"If we are discovered here, we are likely all dead."

"And yet I am riding with Captain Craven, who has escaped from the clutches of death many times," smiled Gramont.

"Even if we could make it out alive after being discovered, the whole operation would fail, and we cannot let that happen."

"Then let us tread quietly."

Gramont walked away, barking his orders in French as if expecting them all to know what he was asking of them.

"What do we do?" Moxy asked in disbelief.

"Follow what they do and try to look like a Frenchman," declared Craven as he climbed onto his horse.

He looked around at the marvellous uniforms of the men around him and then to his own. It was fine attire, but he could not help but feel uncomfortable in it. He had only worn a French uniform once before, but that had been out of necessity in the most desperate of scenarios where he had no choice. He lifted his newly fitted sabre from its scabbard and made a few rotations with the blade to become accustomed to it. It was a large and relatively heavy sabre, but the equally bulky guard balanced it fairly well, and he looked happy enough with it.

Gramont cried out his orders in French, and they didn't need to understand French to know he was calling them into column to begin their march.

"This is most peculiar." Hawkshaw took up position

beside Craven.

"I'm not sure that it is. There is very little that would surprise me in this war anymore," replied Craven wearily.

"Is this not what you came for? Daring adventure?"

"My idea of adventure is not trotting into the middle of a French army and trying to convince them we are in fact Frenchmen also," he groaned.

"But it would be a most fantastic feat if it were to be accomplished, would it not?" he replied with the same kind of excitement Paget so often brought to their endeavours.

"Let's focus on making it happen before we worry about how it will be remembered."

CHAPTER 7

The cavalry troop was passing through a Portuguese village when Craven and the others got to experience first-hand the plight of the locals. It was nearly a ghost town as so many had fled South to Lisbon, as were Wellington's orders, but many could not abandon their homes had stayed behind. The people of the village were wrapped in dirty rags, their winter clothes having been taken from them. Not one of them looked like they had eaten a solid meal in months, and yet they would not look up and make eye contact with those they believed to be Napoleon's troops. As they neared the far side of the village, they could see why the villagers were so terrified of them. One of their own hung from a tree nearby, and a wooden plaque nailed to his body. A short note was scratched into it in their language for all to see.

"Why have they not cut that man down?" Hawkshaw asked in horror.

"He is a reminder to others to not resist the French," replied Ferreira.

Hawkshaw reached for his sword, but Craven reached across. He pressed down on his hand and hilt to keep it in the scabbard.

"Remember who we are supposed to be," whispered Craven, slowly looking around for any prying eyes.

"But this, it is barbaric. Surely, you can see that."

"And if we do anything, the rest of these people here will suffer even more, and we will likely fail in our mission. The best thing we can do for these people is assist Wellington in throwing the French out of the country."

Hawkshaw looked genuinely rattled by the gruesome sight and also distressed he could do nothing about it. They looked back to see two of the villagers glaring back at them in disgust. They looked away so as to not meet the same fate as the man hanging before them. Gramont led them away from the harrowing scene.

"Savages," muttered Hawkshaw.

"I'd like to say we never did it in England, but you must know that we did," said Paget who rode up beside them.

They rode on through a bleak country, with little sign of French troops and a sparse population who avoided them or looked on at them with scorn whenever they met. It was heart wrenching, but none more so than for Hawkshaw who could never have imagined such treatment. He took it as well as Paget would have a year ago, but his time with Craven had tempered him to all manner of things. It was not until the third day they finally encountered French troops as they noted a troop of cavalry on the move. The Frenchmen avoided them completely as if they did not exist, or perhaps they were deliberately avoiding them.

"Deserters do you think?" Hawkshaw asked.

"Likely just soldiers looking for food and avoiding the competition like a fisherman heads for open water," replied Craven.

"You think the army is providing so little for them?"

"I know they are. The French live off the land wherever they go and struggle to provide for their armies far from home. There is little to be found in these lands now."

Another day's ride and they could see the Northern edge of the French position around Santarem, giving them a more accurate perspective of the true scale of the force they had not seen from the South. Gramont drew them to a halt as they looked out across multiple villages and towns, and tent cantonments joining them together in a vast city.

"They remain strong," declared Hawkshaw.

"But for how long?" Paget was imagining the freezing cold winter in which they had endured with far less than those behind the lines.

"I may despise Napoleon, but one must respect the backbone of those who follow him. For most will endure all manner of hardships in his name which many of us would never dream of," replied Gramont.

"So, Colonel, how do we play this?"

"We hold our heads high and move with authority. Let me do the talking. Nobody but my men speak a word whilst we are here. There are very few with the authority to stop our advance."

"And you believe you can convince Masséna of this lie?"

"Captain, I have served France as long as he, and so there

is no lie to hide."

"Except your hatred of Napoleon and his revolutionaries. Masséna rose up from nothing, did he not?"

Gramont nodded in angry agreement.

"You are a relic, Colonel, and perhaps your day will come again, but remember this is a young army, and not the one you once knew. Napoleon has elevated men with nothing to the rank of General, and you must at least pretend to appreciate that fact, or it could cost all our lives. Put your pride aside," insisted Craven.

"It is a lot to ask, but I know I must, and likewise, you must restrain yourself and your men. For I know you must have a great urge to draw cold steel here amongst so many of the enemy."

"I have a great desire to live to see tomorrow, and the sword is not the tool which will achieve that," admitted Craven.

"No, and what is?"

"You are. All of us are only here to give weight to your credibility and defence on the road, but now it all comes down to you. Don't make me regret putting our lives in the hands of a Frenchman."

"And why did you do that?"

"I wasn't given a choice. These were my orders."

"And you are an officer who always follows orders? Is that really so, Captain?"

"When they come directly from Wellington, I do. On our retreat to Lisbon just a few months back, all hoped seemed lost, but Wellington ensured it was not. He has plans set in motion in weeks and months, if not years before they are to be enacted, and so I imagine he has a far better grasp of this than any of us."

"And you? What are your talents, Captain?"

"I think you know very well what they are, Colonel, which is why I am here," smiled Craven.

"Let us move with some urgency, then, Captain, and be out of this danger as quickly as we ride into it."

Craven looked back at his own comrades, seeing the angry face of Birback who was done pretending to be a Frenchman. He looked most uncomfortable in his hussar's uniform.

"Do not look for trouble here, and do not speak. All we need to do is look pretty," he declared to them.

They all looked anxious as they looked towards the thousands of troops ahead of them and knowing there were many more thousands nearby.

"Chin up, Captain, you are one of Napoleon's hussars, act like it!" Gramont roared before digging his heels into his horse and leading them onwards.

The French army was something to behold, even in its starved and wretched state from such a harsh winter. Infantry units still conducted drill whilst others went on with their duties seemingly with little complaint, and they looked up at the approaching cavalry unit with bewilderment. Craven could only imagine the French troops believed they brought good news. Which in a way they did, as they would allow the men to withdraw from such a barren and desolate land which Wellington had starved of nearly every resource on his retreat.

The uniforms Gramont's hussars wore fit in perfectly with those around them, having been captured after hard use or worn and weathered to match. Though they were in a far better state than many of the infantry who wore heavily patched clothing and anything they could find or steal locally. No one greeted

103

them as they progressed past several pickets. There was a grim expression on many of their faces, and nobody dared stop a Colonel at the head of his troop of cavalry. Gramont gave polite gestures as he passed some of them but received a pained and half-hearted response more out of necessity in respect of his rank than any desire to be polite.

"I thought we had it bad," whispered Paget to Craven so quietly it was barely audible over the pounding of the hooves of the horses. Craven merely nodded in agreement, staying silent, as Gramont had requested.

They trotted along for twenty minutes through the French lines before they could see Masséna's headquarters. It was unmistakeable, for all of the officers surrounded it. Craven could feel his pulse racing as he tried to maintain a calm presence for his own troops, and to fool the enemy. As he looked across to his comrades, he could see the terror they hid behind their eyes. None more so than Hawkshaw who looked mortified by what he was seeing. Craven recalled his last encounter with Masséna, but it was out of necessity, not choice. On they rode well past the point of no return, full well in the knowledge there would be no escape if their identity were discovered.

The frequency of troops was getting denser the further they rode, and Gramont soon brought them to a halt. He barked his orders for them to wait for him as he went on alone. Few understood the wording of the orders, but they got his meaning, as the Frenchmen remained in place, and his subordinates and NCOs repeated the order. Many of them dismounted as they moved off of the road, but not Craven.

He enjoyed the vantage point the mount gave him as he looked in on the house that had formed Masséna's headquarters in an amusing mirror of Wellington's. He could see movement through one of the large windows at the front of the house, as heated conversation was underway, but he could not make out any faces. Hawkshaw and Paget stopped beside him so they may talk privately, as Gramont's Frenchmen formed a barrier around those who would never pass as Napoleon's troops were they challenged.

"Do you really trust him, Sir?"

"No, but I figure there is a fifty-fifty chance he is telling the truth."

"And if he is not?" Hawkshaw asked.

"It is too elaborate a plan just to trap a few English troops."

"But not for you," added Paget.

Hawkshaw looked at him in disbelief and bewilderment.

"He cannot be worth so much," he snapped.

"To the right man, absolutely," replied Paget.

Hawkshaw had no comprehension of whom they spoke of, but he could tell from Craven's face it was a legitimate concern.

"Who have you angered this much that he would go so far?"

"You did, and we had never even met for me to have time to offend you."

"I sought out an English officer in Wellington's army. It didn't require any grand feat."

Craven groaned, as he knew he would have to explain.

"Major Bouchard, we have some history over this past year, enough that it feels like a lifetime."

"So, there is a man who wanted to kill you more than me?"

"Many," replied Paget genuinely.

They fell silent as they watched Gramont approach the headquarters and exchange pleasantries with several officers on the way.

"Here we go," muttered Craven wearily.

"How can they not be suspicious of an officer they have never seen nor heard of?" Hawkshaw asked in amazement.

"Do you have any idea how large the armies of France are? I am quite sure many of the Marshals would not even recognise one another," replied Paget.

They all watched intently as the tense situation unfolded before their eyes, and they pretended to be as calm as could be. They heard some discussion nearby and looked across. Two artillery officers were arguing with some of Gramont's troops.

"What do we do?" Hawkshaw asked.

"Nothing we can do, this isn't a time for fighting," whispered Craven.

But he looked more anxious as the discussion became increasingly heated, but he was too far away to understand what was being said.

"Let them ride it out. For none of us can improve that situation."

"Then why did we come?"

"Our work is getting Gramont to and from this camp. For now we are only here to look pretty, so sit up tall and proud."

The artillery officers threw up their hands in disagreement as they walked away to the relief of everyone. Hawkshaw pulled on his reins to go over and see what the commotion was about, but Craven took hold of them, keeping their two horses locked together.

"It doesn't matter. It is resolved."

"Sir, this is it," Paget blurted out excitedly. Craven scowled at him for raising his voice, but he soon turned his attention to the headquarters building where he could see Gramont and Masséna looking out towards their cavalry squadron.

"What are they doing?" Hawkshaw asked quietly.

"I should imagine Masséna wants to be certain Gramont is who he says he is, and that is why we came," whispered Craven, trying to act as casual as he could whilst keeping a keen eye on the window. The two Frenchmen deliberated in a seemingly calm manner.

"I thought he would have been furious to receive this news."

"Perhaps, or maybe he is just relieved to finally be able to withdraw from this disaster," replied Craven.

They seemed deep in conversation when loud activity drew their attention away to the same artillery officers who had hassled their unit before. They had now returned with several comrades, one of which was carrying training sticks not unlike the singlesticks Craven and the Salfords trained with regularly. They began heckling the cavalrymen.

"They are looking for a friendly contest. They ask us to prove we are real men and not just toy soldiers," whispered Hawkshaw.

Birback spat on the ground beside him as he readied himself to fight.

"Nobody moves," insisted Craven.

"You want a frog fighting for us?" Birback snarled.

"Why not?"

"Because we want to win."

"Do we?"

Birback looked stunned at the prospect Craven did not care.

"Remember our mission. All that matters is Masséna believes we are genuine and follows the orders of the message we have delivered," replied Paget.

"And that we get back out alive," added Hawkshaw.

"I think that is rather secondary, at least in the eyes of those who gave us these orders," Craven said.

Birback still tried to turn his horse about to go to the fight, but Craven grabbed hold of his reins.

"Can you convincingly look like a French cavalryman once you've drawn that sabre? How about when they start taunting you, how is your French?"

Birback looked furious but soon backed down as Craven let go. They turned to watch the display as the cavalrymen separated to form an area to fight. One of Gramont's men went forward to take the challenge.

"We shouldn't be doing this," whispered Paget.

"It's a good distraction, I think, and who doesn't want to see two Frenchmen fight?"

Craven smiled, all the while keeping one eye on the headquarters for the first sign of trouble, despite knowing they had no hope of escaping should their worst fears become reality. One of officer's rode up beside them as if to ensure they did not get involved.

"You see that man," he said, pointing to one on the sidelines who had arrived with the gunners and wore civilian attire, "He is a fencing master. The French frequently employ one to many regiments to keep the soldiers in fighting form, something the English would do well to learn from."

"They haven't been doing much of a job," jabbed Birback.

"They train with the sword as a pastime to keep the men fit and in good spirits, but you have spent your whole life fighting," replied Paget in support of the enemy.

"Damn right, I have," agreed Birback.

They watched as the two Frenchman squared off against one another, the gunner upright and with his stick low and directed forward. The cavalryman was in a wider stance, his stick held out in an extended hanging guard, the hilt well above his head, and his shoulders slumped down to be protected by it; the shell up so as to present a small target. The body language alone was enough to show both men had received significant training. They were precise and confident in their posture, covering their lines of defence well in different ways.

"Should be one of us," growled Birback.

"Who cares? Nobody will remember this. That man does not represent us."

"But he does, for now," insisted Birback.

Paget was smiling at him, which made him angrier.

"What?"

"I used to think you were only here for your love of violence, and now I see pride is just as important."

"I just don't like losing," muttered Birback.

One of the Frenchmen called a start to the friendly duel. Each man took a step closer to the other, stopping within a single lunge distance. They maintained their initial guards as though they were frozen in place to pose for a painter. After a few tense moments, the gunner jerked his sword forward just a little to provoke a response, but he did not get it, showing the calm and training possessed by his opponent. The gunner tried once more, committing just a little further this time, but the cavalryman did not respond with a parry as he would have wanted. Instead, he snapped a quick cut around in a circular motion towards his opponent's head. The gunner parried the blow at the very last moment, and a flurry of attacks followed back and forth, as the crowd erupted with cheers at the lively display. The two men went back and forth, and others in the camp soon circled around to see the display of skill. The two fencers struck with such speed and force as though they were trying to split each other's skulls.

"Should we stop this?" Hawkshaw asked.

"Why? This is just what we needed, something which shows that we fit in here."

Craven smiled as he flicked between the fight and the headquarters building when he noticed several officers step out, including Masséna himself with Colonel Gramont by his side. Masséna came forward to watch the battle between the two men, escorted by a dozen of his staff. He looked most amused by the display as they struck back and forth with such vigour. One would think they were bitter enemies were it not for the sticks they engaged with. They carried on for several more minutes without any clean strikes landing until finally as the gunner overreached with a large step in his attack, the cavalryman circled off to one side. He struck him on the knee, causing the man to cry out as his leg gave way. He landed hard on the cold mud to a cheer from the crowd. Even Masséna had gotten into the spirit of it, as Gramont continued to whisper in his ear.

"What is he doing? All he is supposed to do is deliver the

message," grumbled Hawkshaw.

"Gaining his trust. We are asking a lot, and it must be sold with much skill and aptitude," replied Paget.

"And if the old man oversells it?"

"Then we are all dead," replied Craven.

"Our lives are in the hands of a Frenchman?"

"A smart one," admitted Paget as he watched Gramont exchange some coins with officers in Masséna's command. They were taking bets on a wager as to who would win the contest. The gunner was back on his feet in no time and limped for just a few paces, walking off the pain and returning to the fight. The two men cut back and forth with both skill and power for some time before the gunner swung a series of clever feints. He then struck down toward the leg of the cavalrymen in the same place he had been struck, but Gramont's man was too clever and sharp for him. He drew it back, and the stick found nothing but air as he was struck on the top of crown of the head with a smart crack, which echoed out as the crowd cried out in excitement. The stick fell from the gunner's hand as he reached for the gaping wound to find blood gushing down his head. He was initially stunned before bowing our gracefully and accepting defeat.

Masséna cheered with the rest of them, as Gramont smiled and collected his dues, having bet on his own man. He finally shook hands with the Marshal before Masséna left them to return to the warmth of his headquarters. Gramont smiled as he leapt back onto his horse.

"That is it?" Craven asked.

"Yes, though I am to dine with the Marshal this evening, and you will be provided with lodging for the night."

"Lodging? We need to be rid of this place whilst our story still holds true," snapped Hawkshaw.

"And for that to happen we must remain here overnight. What cavalry troop weary from the road would pass up the opportunity of the smallest comfort for the night, and I could not refuse Masséna."

Craven sighed wearily as he knew there was no choice.

"We have been given a barn just a short distance from here where man and beast will find shelter, which is far more than many of these poor souls have." Gramont looked around at the freezing cold and emaciated troops surrounding them, and yet the Colonel waited on Craven's orders.

"We stay tonight, but we set out at first light, and we cannot afford a single mistake this night."

CHAPTER 8

Craven looked out from an open window from the attic of the stables with Paget and Ferreira beside him. They watched as many fires raged in the distance and imagined what might be happening with Colonel Gramont. All of the Salfords and Hawkshaw's men who had travelled with them were at the back of the barn far from contact with any passers-by. Gramont's men relaxed near the barn door and a smaller entrance should anyone come looking for them. Nobody was allowed out.

"I do not like this. I do not like this one bit," insisted Paget.

"None of us do, but Gramont is right. We must do all that we can to avert suspicion and leaving as quickly as we arrived would do us no favours," replied Craven.

"And you believe the Colonel can spend an evening with Masséna and his staff and not draw suspicion once the wine flows?" Ferreira asked.

"I think the truth is there is little to choose between those at the top of Napoleon's staff and those who came before them. The French talk of promotion based on merit, but the truth is there are many wealthy and powerful men who hold positions of power in Napoleon's France."

"Napoleon lives like a king," added Ferreira.

There was a loud and angry knock on the small door to the barn. Craven's hand quickly reached for his sword hilt, ready to draw it, and he got up to fight if necessary. He looked down into the barn to see they were all on edge, readying for a fight without making it look obvious. Two of Gramont's men waited at the door to open it. It was a tense moment for them all, as they expected their deceit to be uncovered at any second.

Gramont's men looked to Craven for instruction as they had been ordered to. He nodded in return, knowing they had no chance but to open the door and face whatever came next. Craven held his breath as the door was pried open calmly, and they pretended to greet whomever it was as if it were any normal day. Some words were spoken between in French, which gave Craven little relief.

"I think…they are bringing us food," whispered Hawkshaw.

The cavalrymen by the door drew back, as ten men carried in bags of food and even a barrel of wine was rolled in for them. Pleasantries were shared amongst the troops bringing the supplies and Gramont's cavalry until finally the men left. The door was shut, at which time they all remained silent and still, as they were both stunned and relieved. Finally, they could wait no longer as a cheer rang out, and they all descended upon the supplies as bread was tossed out from those nearest. Craven looked down in amazement as British and French troops alike mingled to make merry.

"What if it is a trick, Sir? What if they are poisoned?" Paget asked.

"Look around you. If Masséna wanted us dead, there are many easier ways to do it than poison," admitted Craven as he sighed in relief that they had got away with it. Paget went down to join the others and take his fill.

"It is a generous amount to give for an army that starves," declared Ferreira.

"We just gave Masséna the best news he has heard all winter. That he can withdraw to somewhere more hospitable."

A bowl of cuts of pork and bread was soon brought up for them and wine followed. As they sat down to enjoy their meal and make merry, it seemed easy to forget how much danger they were surrounded by. Craven could hear the conversations grow louder as Matthys carried wine to them and could already see the concern on his face. He rushed back downstairs to ensure those not speaking French were near silenced.

"Wine is a dangerous thing to men who must keep their secrets," whispered Paget.

"Yes, but to not drink it would be more suspicious. There is not a Frenchman in this country, let alone our own who would turn down this gift," replied Craven as he gladly stuffed his face.

"Our army survives on so little; I often wonder at the horrors this French army must have experienced."

"I don't have to wonder, I've lived it, and I wouldn't wish it on any man."

"Not even the likes of Major Bouchard?" Ferreira asked.

"No, not even him. A fighting man deserves a chance to

fight or at least a swift death, not to be starved out through a bitter winter."

"And yet we do so to the enemy, deliberately?" Paget asked, knowing that was Wellington's plan.

"I never said it wasn't necessary. We have to win this war, or Napoleon will come for England next, and the whole world will be his. But that doesn't mean I have to like it."

Hawkshaw climbed the ladder and sat down beside them to the surprise of them all.

"What can I do for you, Captain?" Craven asked with suspicion in his voice.

"I only want to know what goes on between the officers of the Salfords who I am attached to. I imagine this is how you plot and scheme and manage all the things you do."

"Sitting around eating and drinking wine? I think you have too high an impression of us."

"He is not wrong," smiled Ferreira.

"But there is never enough wine," shrugged Craven, just as the door of the barn was flung open and another barrel rolled in to a cheer of all inside.

"We don't get treated this well by our own side," muttered Ferreira as the door was slammed shut to prevent the freezing night air coursing in, despite the open window in the attic, at which Paget noticed a thick blanket tied up around the frame to reduce the draft. He got up to release it only to have Craven protest.

"Leave it. If trouble comes our way, I should want to know of it, and there are enough sweaty men in this barn to heat the whole damn thing."

"If trouble comes our way, it won't matter, Sir, you said

yourself." Paget then sat back down.

"No, but I would still rather have a moment's notice than none at all," replied Craven as he downed a cup of wine.

"Do you trust Gramont?" Hawkshaw asked.

"Why would I? A Frenchman I have never met. None of us have any reason to trust him, not until this task is done and without incident."

"Then you gamble a lot."

"Every time I must rely on a man for the first time, only it is rarely at such a great risk," sighed Craven.

The night went on slowly, as not even the wine could relieve them off the fears that they held of being discovered by the enemy at any moment. Yet eventually, they all fell asleep through exhaustion and did not rise until the morning. Craven opened his eyes to see Paget in the open window of the attic, looking out into the street.

"What is it?" Craven growled with a dry throat.

"He has not returned."

"Who hasn't?"

"The Colonel."

Craven suddenly shot awake, adrenaline surging through his veins as he realised what that could mean.

"Matthys, have the horses made ready and every man prepared to move at short notice."

The Sergeant did not hesitate and dropped down the ladder quietly but quickly to relay his orders.

"You expect a morning attack, Sir?"

"It would make sense. With daylight, we would be easy to tackle, and less chance of some of us slipping away under the chaos of darkness," replied Hawkshaw.

"But I thought you said we would be done for if we were discovered here?" Paget asked of Craven.

"Yes, but that is no reason not to try. If we are compromised, you ride like hell and get out of here by any means necessary, you understand?"

"Yes, Sir, but…"

"But nothing. You do not wait for anything. If it comes to it, you ride like the wind, and take Hawkshaw with you. He speaks French well enough it could help."

"And you, Sir?" Paget asked with concern.

"If the enemy know of our identity, then I will be their chief target, and you are both far greater horsemen than I."

"You would sacrifice yourself?" Hawkshaw had expected a more selfish response.

"If this is the trap we feared it might be, there won't be a choice."

"I won't leave without you, Sir," stated Paget sternly.

"You will. There will be no fighting our way out of this if it comes to that. The only way any of us gets out of here is as the fastest a horse can take you, and with all the luck in the world."

"Every man for himself?" Paget sounded disappointed at that.

"There's no point in all of us dying for nothing," replied Hawkshaw.

"But death is not certain, as officers we will be treated with honour."

But Craven shook his head as he pointed to their uniforms.

"Look at us. We are spies, and we will be shot or hanged

for it. Promise me, if the worst happens, you will ride to safety and not look back!"

"I…" began Paget.

"Promise me, I said!"

"I promise," replied Paget in surprise at Craven's aggressive tone.

Hawkshaw looked upon Craven with an open mouth in astonishment.

"What? What's wrong?"

"I…I just always had this image of you in my head. Of how you would be and how you would act. I thought you the most selfish Englishman alive, but…"

"But what?"

Hawkshaw uncharacteristically could not find his words.

"Look," declared Ferreira sternly, but not so loud as to alert any of Napoleon's troops who might be nearby.

They followed Ferreira's gaze to see Colonel Gramont approaching. He was alone and looked a little worse for wear, but in good spirits as he yelled out in French to several of his men at to open the door downstairs.

"He's talking about the night he had, much wine was drunk," translated Hawkshaw.

"Then our identity remains a secret?" Ferreira murmured.

"And the integrity of the orders we delivered remain. We may have done it."

Craven smiled as he leapt onto the ladder to greet the Colonel below, having never been so glad to see a Frenchman in all his life. The Colonel was welcomed with great applause by his own troops, but Craven soon pushed his way through as the door to the barn was shut so they may continue with some privacy.

"What news?"

"Captain, you worry too much," smiled Gramont.

But Craven was not amused.

"Remember whose mission this is. Tell me what happened last night. I must know where we stand," he pressured the Colonel as Gramont embraced several of his countrymen. He finally turned back to address Craven.

"All is well. The orders have been delivered and received, and we are to depart this morning."

But Craven could see from the Frenchman's concerned face that he had not revealed all.

"And?"

"Our work here is successful, Captain. That is all that matters."

"You discovered something else?"

Gramont nodded in agreement as he took the Captain aside so they may whisper quietly in privacy.

"Messengers are being sent to Cairo."

"What? Why?"

"Napoleon has used many Mamluks in his service, and I imagine he seeks many more, or perhaps from the Ottoman Turks or Albanians, who are all much hardened by war. I do not know the full meaning of the mission, only that it appears to be of great importance. If Napoleon could raise an army there, he may not need to his armies in Portugal and Spain to join together to a force far greater than anything your Lord Wellington can muster."

"But the Royal Navy, how would the French move such a force?"

"They can only cover so much of the coast of this peninsula. They would stop any such force passing Gibraltar, but once landed in Spain, what could we do?" Ferreira joined in with the conversation.

"The French fortresses still hold out," replied Paget in hope.

"Badajoz is weeks from falling and may have already," growled Craven.

"This is a concern for another day, Captain. We have successfully delivered our message and not been discovered. Let us leave with this victory," insisted Gramont.

Craven snapped back to the reality of the vast threat surrounding them.

"Mount up. We move out, now," he snapped as he went for his horse.

"Was it all still worth it?" Paget asked as they climbed into the saddles together.

"Yes, we knew more was to come. What matters is we dealt with our orders. If England would have us leave this country, none of it mattered anyway."

"We've done what we set out to do, and we should take the victory for what it is," added Hawkshaw.

Craven begrudgingly nodded in agreement.

"Now let us be gone, for I would wear this uniform not a minute longer than I must," declared Craven.

The barn doors were swung open, and the troop rode out calmly, doing their best to hide their triumphant victory. Masséna himself and several of his staff had ridden up to see them off and shared a few words with Gramont. Craven watched carefully, expecting a trap to be sprung. Although after a few pleasantries, they were back on the road, making their way past thousands of enemy troops. It was a disconcerting experience, but also a relief to know they were now heading away from the army and not into the centre of it. After some time, they finally left the last of the French pickets and rode out into open ground, but they had ridden for only ten minutes when Moxy called out to alert Craven that galloping riders approached from the rear. He wheeled his horse about to see five French troops approaching on horseback.

"Have they discovered us?" Hawkshaw asked.

"If they had, the whole army would be snapping at our heels," replied Paget.

But as they drew nearer, they recognised the officer and one of his men as those who had challenged them to a contest the day before.

"What do they want?" Craven asked Gramont whilst they were still approaching.

"Likely a renewed contest, and perhaps a rather more serious one," admitted the Frenchman.

Craven looked around to see they were in a quiet area, but they could still see some of the French pickets far into the distance.

"We will entertain them on the far side of that ridge." Craven was looking North to a position that would conceal them from anyone who cared to be watching from afar.

"You would risk everything now after we have achieved all we came for?"

"They come looking for a fight, Colonel, and I would not have them disappointed."

The French artillerymen approached, an officer, a

sergeant, and three of their gunners, all on horseback. The officer cried out in French. He was angry and yet playful at the same time. Gramont quickly relayed Craven's orders, and the artillery officer eagerly accepted, as the two parties moved to the position of privacy and began to dismount fifty paces from one another.

"The officer asks he fight an equal of ours."

"He's mine," growled Ferreira.

His response garnered concern from many, but the Portuguese Captain was quick to explain himself.

"This is my country they destroy. I held my tongue as we passed through towns and villages and saw my people hanged by the neck."

"And when they discover you are no Frenchman?" Paget whispered.

"I do not care if they do!" Ferreira stripped away his tunic, drew out his sabre, and went forward to accept the challenge before anyone could stop him.

"Are we going to let this happen, Sir?"

"It already is happening," replied Craven who didn't seem at all bothered by the prospect.

Gramont oversaw the contest as he shared some words in French with them, to which Ferreira merely nodded in agreement with a cold and murderous expression on his face.

"They fight until one submits or is unable to continue," translated Hawkshaw.

"Then it is to the death?" Paget looked to Craven to intervene. But his gaze remained fixed on the two combatants as they took up their guards, and Gramont signalled for them to begin.

The French artillery officer leapt forward eagerly with a big smile upon his face, testing Ferreira's defence with some quick but short strikes to each side. Ferreira's cavalry sabre was a handful compared to what he preferred to use, but he twirled it about as if were half the weight it truly was; much to the surprise of the Frenchman who got a taste for Ferreira's skill before a blow had even been launched toward him. He tried again with some more determined attacks as Ferreira remained on the defensive, absorbing everything that was thrown at him with ease. Until the smile faded from the Frenchman's face as he realised the deep water he had gotten himself into.

One great lunge caused him to overstep as Ferreira nimbly circled out of the way. The Frenchman's foot slid out from under him so that he dropped down onto one knee. Ferreira waited for him to get up and turned to face him before they continued.

"And now it is my turn," he whispered, causing the French officer's eyebrows to raise in horror at the realisation he was not fighting a fellow Frenchman. He could say and do nothing about it as he was forced to defend himself. Ferreira went at him with a flurry of precise but powerful blows, putting more of the shoulder in than he normally would so as to batter the man's sword aside, and both tire and humiliate him. In his anger, Ferreira missed one quick disengage. The point of the man's sword drove into his thigh just a fingernail's length, as he stopped himself going forward and driving it deeper. He grabbed it, pulling it out of his body before continuing his attack. He cut under at the Frenchman's arm and cut deeply, following up with a powerful batter of his blade, slashing across his chest. It caused him to fall to one knee as he dropped his sword.

He was beaten, but Ferreira closed the distance, took his sabre in two hands, and drove it down into the officer's body. It killed him instantly. He pulled out the blade, causing blood to spew out over his uniform. He then looked at the Frenchman's companions as if they were next. The sergeant reached for his sword, but before he could get the blade clean from the scabbard, a blistering volley of fire rang out from Ferreira's Portuguese comrades. They had kept their carbines and pistols at their sides ready to use. The scene of the duel became a thick cloud of powder fog for a few moments.

There were no cheers or celebrations, but also no protests, not even from Matthys, who shied away from unnecessary violence at all times.

"This was unnecessary," whispered Paget in horror.

"I don't think any of us can presume to know how we would react after seeing the things they have seen happen to their own country and people," admitted Matthys.

Craven went forward to see the devastation for himself as the cloud of powder smoke began to clear. He had no words for Ferreira, as he had a lot of sympathy for the Portuguese situation, having seen the same horrors with his own eyes. He drew out his sword as he went to the bodies of the Frenchmen. None were still breathing, having all been hit by multiple shots.

"If we are suspected of this, it could endanger everything we have done."

"Craven nodded in agreement with Gramont.

"Take the horses and weapons and anything of value. This was a guerrilla attack, do you understand?" Craven barked.

Birback was the first amongst them, looking for anything of value as they began to strip the bodies.

"Let's go, for we have already outstayed our welcome!" Craven roared.

"And yet this is my country." Ferreira wiped his blade off in his tunic his adversary had taken off just moments before.

"It was, and it will be once again, but all in good time. Soon we will come out of winter, and everything will change." Craven patted his friend on the shoulder in solidarity.

"Did you have to kill that man? Did you have to kill all of them?" Hawkshaw was looking at the brutal devastation before them.

"Did you have to come here to Portugal?" Craven snapped at him.

"You came to a war looking for blood. Do not be surprised when you find plenty of it," declared Paget who was no stranger to it anymore.

They mounted up and rode on, leaving the bodies for the enemy to find. They were soon passing through Portuguese villages and towns where those who had remained looked at them with disgust for the uniforms they wore, and yet that made Hawkshaw feel less sorrow for the bodies they had left in their wake.

"Someday soon we will return to this place, and it will be flying our own colours," declared Craven as they rode on.

It was a grim few days' travel as they wondered if the enemy would discover their identity and pursue them. They kept watch every night in fear of the same Bandidos and guerrillas who they had fought beside so many times, and now stalked them. But it was the sight of the Sampson that calmed their nerves as they returned to the uniforms they had hidden, and finally stripped away the French ones they had been so eager to dispose of. They stepped up to the beach and began to load the boats for their return journey.

"We really did it, didn't we? We tricked a Marshal of France?" Hawkshaw smiled.

"A Marshal of Napoleon, not of France," corrected Gramont who was quick to remind everyone that the Emperor did not speak for every Frenchman.

"Now what, Sir?" Paget asked.

"We have just made sure the war can go on for another year."

"Is that a good thing?" Hawkshaw asked.

"They are the invaders here. The longer this war goes on, the better our chances."

"How? How can that be whilst we fight so far from home?"

"Because it is not just us fighting. The people of Portugal and Spain fight their invaders at every turn. You just have not seen it yet," replied Paget.

"And yet all I hear of is Spanish armies and Spanish cities falling."

"It is true. There is not a Spanish or Portuguese army who can stand against the armies of Napoleon. That job falls to us, but do not underestimate all that is done here. The work and the fighting that happens far from your eyes or any redcoat. These operations far from friendly soil, this is everyday life for many of the people of this place. We may eventually beat the likes of Masséna in open battle, but he will be ground down to dust so that we fight a mere shadow of a French army," admitted Craven.

They boarded the vessel feeling a mix of triumphant

return but also fear for the coming weeks and months. They watched the beautiful coastline from the deck of the Sampson as they set sail without any pomp or ceremony. For none of the crew could know the meaning of their mission nor the result of it. Hawkshaw approached Craven who was leaning over the gunwale deep in thought.

"Is this what it is like? Is this how Captain Craven wages war?"

"Sometimes. It is whatever it needs to be. The only certainty is that I will fight, and that I know I have friends who will have my back."

Hawkshaw sighed as he leaned in over the side beside Craven.

"What?"

"It's hard hating you. It was easy when we were hundreds or thousands of miles apart."

"Really? Plenty of men find it quite easy," smiled Craven.

"I thought I knew what I came here for, but I don't know anymore. But one thing I am sure of, I didn't come for this. Sneaking around in the clothes of the enemy and pretending to be something I am not. It is not for me. I must leave all this madness behind."

"Then what will you do?"

"I have my duties with the Portuguese army, and I shall return to that position and continue it to the utmost of my ability. If I am to fight this war, it will be at the front of a body of fine soldiers on the field of battle."

"Then I wish you every luck."

Hawkshaw looked suspicious as if he were being tricked.

"I have no quarrel with you, Captain, except when you

attempt to take my life."

CHAPTER 9

Craven and Gramont were waiting before Wellington's desk as he quietly discussed a few matters with Spring and another two officers in the corner of the room. The Frenchman looked at Craven to see they were both as anxious to hear whether their efforts had borne fruit, but they were being made to wait. Finally, Wellington paced over to his desk and sat down with a comforting sigh.

"Gentlemen, we have confirmed reports from Major Thornhill that there has been quite the bonfire at Santarem. The boats destined to be used for a crossing of the Tagus have gone up in flames, and so your mission was a complete success," he smiled.

"Well done, both of you," added Major Spring.

"And now you will advance North and defeat Masséna?" Gramont asked impatiently.

"All in good time, Major. For we move slowly but steadily

to victory, and gamble as little along the way as possible," insisted Wellington.

Gramont look frustrated but nodded in agreement.

"Now, what is it I hear of Cairo?" Wellington demanded before they had even had a moment to celebrate their successes.

"Whatever Napoleon's intentions are in Egypt, or any of his Marshals, I fear he will get little response, or at least not the kind they would expect," replied Gramont.

"You leave that concern to us." Major Spring seemed rather more worried about the prospect.

"Is it not a desperate move to look for troops in Cairo?" Craven asked.

"Or does it show a relentless will to go on fighting here?" replied Wellington.

"Egypt is not my concern. France is my concern," snapped Gramont.

"Then you will share all that you know of operation and be on your way, Sir," snarled Wellington.

* * *

Moxy filled a bowl of steaming stew for Paget. He took a large piece of bread from a nearby table and sat down beside the fire where their food was prepared. The Salfords had gathered around many fires as they delved into a good meal, relieved to be reunited with their comrades and able to enjoy a meal without looking over their shoulders.

"That was a hell of a thing," he admitted to Charlie as she sat down beside him. She looked even angrier and put out that she had been left behind than when she had first heard the disappointing news.

"I should have been there!"

"Should you? Do you think you could have remained calm amid ten thousand French troops? Do you think you could have worn their uniform without attracting attention?" Matthys asked.

"You do not trust me to do what is needed?" She looked to Paget for support but did not find it.

"But you thought he was up to the task?" She pointed to the crude Birback who lapped from his bowl like a dog.

"It was for the best," insisted Paget.

"You think I cannot put my personal feelings aside, and the rest of you can?"

Paget shied away from the answer as he peered over to Ferreira and immediately drew her suspicions.

"Then it was not all plain sailing without me, was it?"

"You didn't see what we saw," replied Matthys.

"Didn't see what you saw? I have seen what the French do more than any of you."

She slammed her wooden bowl down at Matthys' feet, causing some of it to splash over his boots.

"This is how it is to be now?" she demanded of Paget.

But when she got no answer, she stormed away, causing Birback to reach for the bowl she had thrown to extract the dregs that were left as though he was a starving beggar. Paget went to get to his feet, but Matthys calmly exclaimed. "Leave it," causing him to sit back down. For he knew Matthys was the calming presence and counsel so often needed, and yet so often ignored at a cost to them all.

"Craven was right to leave Charlie behind, but that doesn't

make it any more palatable."

"And now she hates us for it," sobbed Paget.

"Only for a little while. Imagine how you would feel upon the triumphant return of your comrades when you were intentionally left behind."

"I wonder how you ever came to be a soldier," smiled Paget in reply to his sobering and insightful thoughts.

"I never should have been, but these days have made many of us into something we never thought possible. England has never known war on this scale. I am what I am needed to be."

"Is that what you think of us, too? Is that why you did not protest what we did up North, when Craven was doing the same drove a wedge between you," added Ferreira.

"It is different. What you did, and what we all do here is ugly business, but Craven spilled English blood where there should never have been a need to, or at least I thought as much at the time. But what you did against the enemy, it is war. Were we to be discovered by the enemy at any time during that mission, we would have been put to death, and so there is no shame in killing when you risk being killed."

"Even when we wear the uniform of the enemy and are little more than spies?" Paget asked.

"No war was ever won by being good and playing fair."

"Can that argument be used to justify almost anything?"

"No, we do what we must. We kill because we must, not because we enjoy it."

"I am not sure that is true of all of us." Paget looked to Birback who merely smiled back.

"We will all be judged for what we have done, and I fear

he will surely go to hell. But I think he already knows that," replied Matthys.

"Then I'll be in good company!" Birback roared with seemingly no care at all.

"You're already in better company than you deserve!" Craven returned, causing Paget to jump to his feet to greet him.

"What news, Sir?"

"The good news is our mission was a complete success and achieved all that could be hoped," replied Craven, leaving them anxious for the bad news.

"But we are not done yet, Sir?"

"Our work in Portugal is done for now, but our path now lies elsewhere."

He had piqued all their interest, but for different reasons as Ferreira came angrily forward.

"Our work is not done here. Where else can we possibly be needed?" he demanded as all the officers and NCOs, as well as Craven's closest friends gathered around.

"The French sent a diplomatic mission to Cairo in search of troops to bolster them here in Portugal and Spain."

"What concern of that is ours?" Ferreira asked.

"A great one if they return with an army."

"It has fallen to us to stop them, Sir?" Paget appeared fascinated at the prospect.

"Yes, it has that."

"But why? What do you know of Egypt?"

Craven took a deep breath as he knew what came next would be a lot to stomach, particularly for Ferreira.

"Major Thornhill's spies have it on good authority that amongst the French mission is a certain Major Bouchard."

"And so you volunteered so you could fight him once more?" Ferreira snapped angrily.

"No, I did not volunteer anything. Major Thornhill believes that I, as one of the few British officers to have met Bouchard face to face and with so much of an intimate connection, am best suited to hunting him."

"Hunt? You want to hunt the most dangerous man we have ever met in all the world?" Ferreira was furious, having seen first-hand the long journey it took for Craven to recover from their previous encounters.

"Frankly, I am one of the only officers who can identify Bouchard, and we are also uniquely suited to this kind of mission."

"What kind of mission?" Matthys pressed.

"A small and quiet one. Just a handful of men."

"You cannot be so naive to think this is anything short of a death sentence?" Ferreira asked.

"A small unit gathering intelligence when they have no idea we have knowledge of them, it could work," admitted Matthys.

"It is madness," protested Ferreira.

"This is not up for discussion!"

They were all silenced and he went on, first addressing his closest Portuguese friend.

"I wouldn't ask you to leave your country at its greatest time of need, but know that neither do I abandon it, nor you. We go to Egypt to secure the future for us all."

Ferreira nodded in acceptance and a little relief that he was not being forced to leave his homeland. Craven then continued.

"A small number of us will travel to Cairo. We will do

what we can to discover the ambitions of this French mission, and if possible, disrupt any plans they might have. We are in the last throws of winter, and little should happen here in the coming weeks. Ferreira, I am leaving you in command. I will only take volunteers, but Mr Paget, you will be most valuable if you would come, for you are a gentleman and possess certain skills the rest of us do not."

"Of course, Sir."

"You won't leave me behind a second time," declared Charlie.

Craven nodded in appreciation.

Matthys put up his hand to volunteer, which was never in doubt.

"It beats sitting around here freezing my bollocks off," Birback laughed.

"You'll need a good shot," Moxy said.

"I believe I might be of some assistance," added Caffy, having gained much experience as both a slave and as a free man.

"And I've always wanted to see it, Cairo," admitted Joze.

Craven nodded in appreciation that his closest friends were backing him, to see Hawkshaw and Benning step up to join them.

"What happened to treading your own path as a cavalryman?"

"Orders happened. As a fluent French speaker, I am to join you on this mission," admitted Hawkshaw in frustration.

"And him?" Paget pointed to Benning.

"I would travel with someone who would have my back, and there is nobody you would want to have by your side when you find trouble than him."

"When do we depart, Sir?" Paget asked.

"Immediately, we are to meet Major Thornhill at the port in two hours, and so we must be on our way shortly."

"And the Salfords, what are we to do?" Ferreira asked.

"Keep training and get plenty of rest. When the spring comes, there will be much work to be done."

Ferreira looked relieved to be able to rest easy, as Craven went for his horse, having not gotten a moment's rest. Paget rushed to catch up as he mounted Augustus, who he had missed greatly during their mission in the North.

"Would a night's rest not be wise, Sir?"

"We may rest aboard the ship we travel. We do not know how much of a lead the French party has on us, and I would not waste any time."

Anticipation was high as they wondered what they were getting themselves into. The journey to the port went by quickly, as they arrived just two hours before sundown. They tied up their horses beside a small warehouse as Thorny ushered them inside. On the shelves and counters around them was all manner of clothes and equipment. It appeared as a wardrobe for a theatre production.

"What are we doing here?"

"You will not travel as soldiers of the British Army, none of you. You are not travelling under our flag nor orders."

"And without the protection of the Army and Navy, Sir?" Paget asked in horror.

"As civilians you will not be a target, except for thieves and brigands, and you may stay plenty well armed enough to deal with them."

"What are we supposed to be?" Craven asked.

"You will travel aboard the Margaretta with Captain Payne under the guise of an American merchant vessel in search of new trade contacts in the slave trade."

"Payne? That bastard?"

"My understanding is last time you were together you saw off a French privateer together?"

"Yes," Craven said, as he remembered the hardship and how difficult Payne had been.

"Now, shed everything that identifies you as English troops. That means everything, from weapons to uniforms to regulation shoes. Nobody must look at you and even think for one moment you are taking the King's shilling."

Paget looked to Craven in horror, but the Captain took off his sword belt and looked at the gleaming gilt regulation hilt. His sword was far from any normal officer's sword, but it was still unmistakably British. He placed it down on a countertop, along with his dirk but looked on at his double-barrelled pistol with fondness, having recently recovered it from Bouchard.

"That you can keep. It looks like just the kind of thing an American rogue would carry. Well, come on, get to it!"

They begrudgingly stripped off everything but their shirts and underwear, dressing themselves in a broad mix of civilian clothing of varying cut and quality. Craven reached for a slot hilt spadroon of the sort not carried by British troops for almost twenty years.

"Admiral Nelson had a sword just like it as a young man, Sir! I've seen such a painting!" Paget declared with excitement.

Craven drew the sword from its scabbard and looked at the spine. It was marked JJ Runkel of Solingen, a high quality German blade manufacturer that was commonly used by a great many of the top sword cutlers in Britain. It was a robust weapon for its type and of high quality, despite its simple and undecorated hilt, of which the brass work was near black from a lack of polish. Yet the blade was clean and well oiled. He took a large knife to accompany it and pulled on a three-quarter length black coat over a very dark green waistcoat, which made Paget smile.

"What?"

"You look like a pirate, Sir."

"Do pirates have a look?"

He took a faded top hat to complete his look but could not help but feel peculiar as he put it on. He realised how accustomed he had become to his military uniform, as if his body had forgotten all else. The rest of them were soon fully clothed and equipped. They no longer looked like a military unit, but a bunch of cutthroat traders. Moxy had found a long barrel American rifle, which he was most content with, as Birback settled on a pair of tomahawk axes in favour of a sword. Paget took a robust smallsword of the colichemarde type, with the first third of the blade by the hilt as wide as a cavalry sabre, despite the rest being a nimble stabbing implement.

"Listen up!" Major Thornhill roared now that they were ready.

They all gathered around looking like a motley crew that any sensible person would stay well clear of.

"Your mission is to discover the intentions of the French mission in Cairo, and if possible, put a stop to it by any and all means necessary."

"Any?" Matthys asked.

Thorny nodded in agreement. "We have no friends in

Cairo now. All that matters is that you stop the French gaining reinforcements from the region, so do whatever you must, but remember, you have no one to rely on. No one will come to your rescue. Should you encounter any major difficulties, Captain Payne will not hesitate in sailing away and going on about his business without giving you another thought."

"And if we find Major Bouchard?"

"Kill him. You know the damage he can do. If there is one man I wish dead more than any other, it is him."

"Even above Napoleon?" Benning joked.

"His time will come. Now remember, whilst you are out there, you are not soldiers. You will not use ranks, and you will not act or speak in a soldierly manner. That said, Craven is in charge, and Paget after him. Do what you can but remember where you are. Cairo is a dangerous place. A three-way conflict exists which I cannot even begin to explain to you, even if I did understand it myself. Keep your wits about you. The only things keeping you safe are the weapons you carry and the prospect of bringing trade. I wish I could tell you more. I wish I had more information to share with you. In all honesty, this could be nothing more than a fruitless endeavour, or it could be a most deadly one. Do what you can, but do not die for nothing."

Craven pointed for them to go on, and they left the warehouse until only he and Thorny remained in the doorway. They looked out to the port towards the ship he now recognised as the one that would carry them across to Africa, a distant and exotic land the likes of which Craven could never have imagined himself travelling to.

"You don't much rate this mission, do you?"

"It is a fool's errand based on intelligence provided by a

single French royalist. I do not know whether he is to be trusted, and I have heard nothing of these plans with my network of spies. Perhaps in some days or weeks I may hear something, but then it might be too late."

"You don't trust Major Gramont?"

"Of course, I do not, do you?"

"More than I did a week ago, but not so much that I would gamble my life on."

"Then go to Cairo. Find something or find nothing, but make sure you come back alive."

"I didn't know you cared so much for us?" Craven smiled.

"You are a weapon, Craven, the likes of which an officer such as myself would not be without. This war here in Portugal has ground to a halt, as we knew it would. But the time to move will come again soon, and I would have you here when that happens. You are not a subtle or fine implement, but a most valuable one, Captain. I wish you good luck," he said, handing Craven a large and heavy bag of coins.

He left without another word as Craven went forward to join his small party. He found Paget looking back at Augustus who was still tied up.

"What of our horses, Sir?"

"We travel without them. No American merchant would sail with horses. We shall acquire what we need on arrival, but don't worry. Major Thornhill will see to Augustus and the others."

Craven led them on towards the Margaretta. As they approached, they could see the vessel still bore the scars of their encounter with the French privateer. Only that which needed to function had been repaired or replaced. Any cosmetic damage had been ignored entirely, with musket balls lodged in the upper hill and other splintered damage. They stepped aboard to find a few hands on deck, and Captain Payne sitting idly, smoking a clay pipe and a bottle of sherry in his other hand.

"Captain Craven." He smiled as he took a swig from the bottle and followed it with a draw on his pipe, "I truly hope your pay from King George is worth all that you do for him," he smirked.

"You know it isn't, Captain."

"Then why bother? You do not do this out of duty, so why? Why will you sail across to Africa and risk everything when the war is here?"

"I want to kill a man," admitted Craven as he used a half-truth to sell their story. Payne took another draw on his pipe, studying Craven's face and contemplating his answer. He finally bursting out into a booming laughter and got to his feet.

"Now that is a cause I can get behind!" He paced towards Craven and slapped him on the back in admiration for the seemingly simple and primal instincts of his quest.

"And these boys will follow you to such an end?"

"We are with the Captain wherever he goes!" Paget yelled.

"Tell me, have you ever been to Cairo? Have you ever dealt with the Ottomans, or the Mamluks? What about the Albanian mercenaries?"

Paget shook his head at the Captain's question.

"Cairo is a cutthroat place for those who live there, let alone strangers. You better be sure you have coin to bribe and blade to wield against those you cannot bribe, or you will be buried there."

Paget looked horrified at the prospect. It was a reminder

of how he felt as he rode through Portugal in the uniform of a French soldier, glared upon with murderous intent.

"You will take us to Cairo and wait to bring us back here, but nothing more, is that right?" Craven asked.

"That is what I have been paid for. I am not here to risk my neck or my ship for you nor King George," smiled Payne.

"I would expect nothing more," muttered Paget.

But Payne's expression turned from amusement to anger at his words.

"I gave up everything for your king and look where it got me. If England had put half the effort into the Americas as you are here in Portugal, then I would never have had to leave my home."

"And perhaps if more Americans had enough backbone to stand against worthless rebels, you would never have had to leave," snapped Paget.

Payne looked angry for a moment as he looked to the others for a response before finally bursting out into laughter.

"All right, I'll help you sail to your deaths. Let us get you started!"

CHAPTER 10

Craven awoke swinging in his hammock. For despite how tired his body was his mind was a hive of activity. The splash of the hull bobbing in the sea and the creak of the planks irritated him as he was on edge. It gave him restless legs, and he had no choice but to get up and go on deck to get some fresh air to help pass the time. It was still dark, but the glow of the morning sun was already appearing on the horizon.

"I did not imagine you to be an early riser," declared Captain Payne as he approached.

"Not when I have solid ground under me."

Though he knew even that was not true anymore as so much weighed on his troubled mind.

"How long until we reach Cairo?"

Payne smiled at his impatience, having been at sea for less than a day.

"The Margaretta is a fast ship, and we move swiftly on

these winds, but it will be twelve days or more before we reach our destination."

Craven shook his head.

"What has that bastard got us into?" he muttered.

"I used to work for men like Major Thornhill, and I can tell you they have no care for the risks you take. A man like that would send you out to die for any chance of gaining the most modest of information."

"And so what, I should go it alone, like you?"

Payne shrugged as if to agree.

"If you had made your riches, you wouldn't be out here taking scraps from the likes of Major Thornhill."

"Well that rather depends on what you consider to be riches. I have a ship, and a crew I can mostly rely on. I am free."

"Free of what?"

"Free to go and do as I please. I have done my time fighting for a king and a flag, and I can tell you it was not worth it."

"And if the crown had won, if the Americas were still under the King? Would it have been worth it then?"

"Don't tell me you are out here for the King?"

Craven shook his head.

"I'll fight for those beside me, and I'll fight to stop the French invading England. I'll even fight for the Portuguese and Spanish people; heaven knows they need it."

"Why? I bet you were never a man who was compelled to serve and to fight for the King."

"We all go looking for meaning in our lives. I don't think many find it."

"And you have?"

"Maybe a little, his name is Major Bouchard."

"And when you find this Major and you end him, what then?"

"I could say the same for you. After you have done this job and been paid, what then for you?"

"I go on living, that is the difference. No matter what happens in Cairo, you will just go on serving endlessly until you are killed or invalided out. I bet you think you will live forever," smirked Payne.

"We both know you could die just as easy out here wearing no uniform at all, Captain."

"Perhaps, but at least I will have the pleasure to do it on my own terms."

"Clearly you don't know me well enough," replied Craven in his own defence.

"The great free spirit that is James Craven. So free he follows his orders like a good little soldier," ridiculed Payne.

Craven opened his mouth to respond before looking into Payne's face to see he was leading him on, and they both burst into laughter.

"So, tell me what you know about Cairo?" Craven finally asked.

Payne took a deep breath as he considered the complex scenario.

"Egypt was once the pinnacle of civilisation, and I think one day it might be so again. The old battles the new. The Mamluks were a dominant force for hundreds of years, and despite being well diminished, they remain a strong force. Wealthy and decadent, they wear gold and jewels all about their bodies, but do not underestimate them. They are fearsome warriors. The Ottomans officially rule the country, but so far from their reach they have little influence. Perhaps the most powerful man is the Viceroy Muhammad Ali. He is a forward thinker. He sends out people all across Europe to learn and bring back skills and knowledge. He would see Egypt become a great Empire once more."

"How do you know all of this?" Craven was surprised that a seemingly crass American would have so much knowledge of a distant land.

"If you trade in these waters, you do well to know who is powerful, who is wealthy, and who is dangerous."

"And this Ali, and the people of Cairo, are they a threat to us?"

Payne laughed. "There are threats around every corner in Cairo. Thieves, brigands, and anyone who does not like the look of you, you will soon see."

"And the powers in charge? What of them?"

"Hard to say, but it would not be wise to wear a British nor a French soldier's coat there. For they have not forgotten the war brought to their lands by both only a few years ago, though I suspect they hold a greater grudge against Napoleon than your lot."

"Ours you mean."

"I might have fought for the crown in the revolution, but there are times when being an American has its benefits. I claim no part in this conflict."

"And yet here you are transporting English troops."

"No, that is not technically true. I carry travellers who wear no uniforms, and your business is your own."

"And if we get into trouble out there you, you won't come

to our aid, will you?"

"The only reason I fight is to defend this ship and what's on board. I don't owe anyone a thing!"

"I suspect you were not always like that."

"I was young and foolish once, I have to admit, but those days are long behind me."

"I don't believe that is true."

"No? And why not?"

"A man might make a great deal of money operating a ship like this, particularly in these past few years. There must have been more work than you could ever hope to take and at good prices. A man might retire and live a great life with a fine estate after only a few years of work like that."

Payne smiled as though to acknowledge if not admit it.

"Then you are just like the rest of us, still trying to find what we are looking for before we die," sighed Craven.

"I think you found exactly what you wanted."

Craven looked surprised, as he wasn't sure of it himself.

"Adventure and excitement. I can see it in your eyes, and I know because I was once like you, and maybe a little of that still remains. Perhaps that is why I am still out here and not laid up somewhere and resting easy." Payne looked longingly to the horizon as the sun rose.

"So, when I enter Cairo, who can I trust?"

"Trust no one. Nobody will be on your side without payment, and even then, they are just as likely to take your money and run or try and kill you to take whatever else you have. You are foreigners in a faraway land, and those clothes may hide your identity but not your riches. Men who travel with such fine swords are not poor. They will certainly see that."

Craven looked down at the sword dangling by his side and the arsenal they would be carrying between them. It had never occurred to him that such well armed men would be such a target.

"Do you believe the French could find support there?"

Payne shrugged.

"I know what I need to know to get by, make a profit, and survive the experience. I think the different factions in Egypt have their hands full with their own feuds, but I also know that sizeable sums of money and the promise of military aid can be powerful motivators."

Paget and several of the others stepped up onto the deck. Payne went about his business as he began to bark orders to a number of the crew.

"You are up early, Sir?" Paget asked in concern.

"I'd give anything to sleep on solid ground," he sighed.

"What are we to do, Sir? For it could be two weeks until our arrival I fear."

Craven looked around for some idea when his eyes fixed on Joze and the large knife he always carried in his belt. He was one of the few amongst them who could keep his treasured weapon, as it gave no indication that he served in the army. Craven was reminded of the dangerous and violent potential of Cairo and realised Joze would be quite at home there. He looked back to Paget.

"What do you know about fighting with a knife, Lieutenant?"

"A knife, Sir? Why would one fight with a knife? That is a tool for daily activities or slitting throats, not one I need ever concern myself with."

"And when you are attacked with one? What will you do?"

"Why, I shall defend myself with my sword, Sir."

"And if you do not have your sword to hand? What if you have no time to draw it? What if it is taken from you or lost? Then what will you do?"

"I…I…" Paget hesitated as if terrified by the prospect that he never would have imagined being a possibility.

"You have learned to use a sword and your fists quite well, but in a dirty street fight, what will you do about a knife?"

"I don't know, Sir."

"Joze, I imagine you have had plenty of use for that knife long before you ever joined this army."

"I do not wear it as jewellery," he smirked.

"Moxy, find me two small staves the size of that dagger you carry."

Paget sighed as he realised what was going on.

"You would have us learn to fight like thieves? Surely not, Sir?"

"I would have you survive an encounter with one who does. This is what is expected of us. Wellington has sent us to a most dangerous place where we are not protected by the army nor your rank or uniform. We may walk into a den of vipers in a few days' time, and the only thing to protect us is what we can do with our own hands. You have learned to fight as a gentleman and as a soldier, and I will admit you have excelled as both, but now you must learn to fight like a devil."

"This is what we will lower ourselves to? What honour is there in it?" Paget demanded angrily.

"There is honour in winning, and there is honour in completing the mission set us. There is no honour nor glory in dying in a distant land for nothing."

"I only need my sword and my wits."

But it was Charlie who squared off against him. She paced across the deck and stopped ten paces from him, her hand on the knife in her belt, and looking at him with murderous intent.

"Prove it," she insisted.

"Prove what?"

"Prove to me that all you need is your sword and your wits. Just as you said."

"Yes!" Birback roared excitedly as the challenge was issued, hoping for blood, or at least some entertainment.

Paget looked to Craven to save him from the madness he perceived, but it was clear the Captain was quite content to see it play out, and several of Payne's crew stopped their chores to watch also.

"Like Charlie says, let's see you prove you can do what needs to be done with that sword of yours."

Paget turned back to Charlie. She was glaring at him intensely as if they had never met before, and he was merely an easy mark for her as a backstabbing thief. Craven pulled out a handkerchief from his pocket.

"When this touches the deck, you may both draw."

Paget began to sweat as Craven extended his arm, and both he and Charlie kept one eye on it and another on each other. The whole crew had fallen so quiet; the only thing that could be heard was the creaking of the ship's boards and the cutting of the bow through the water.

Craven let the light cloth go, and it descended gently, causing the tension to grow further. Finally, it touched the wet deck. Paget reached for his sword, but Charlie leapt forward and had her knife in hand from the first step. He fumbled slightly as his fingers knocked the ward iron of his sword, and he lost a fraction of a second before his fingers got a hold of his grip. It was already too late. She was on top of him, pressing down on the pommel of his sword to keep it locked in its sheath whilst presenting her own blade to his throat.

It was a sobering and humbling experience for Paget as many cheered at Charlie's victory before going about their business. Charlie sheathed her weapon and stepped away.

"Few are so quick," declared Paget in his defence.

"You can't make that argument when you're dead," replied Craven.

Paget looked for support, but he found none amongst a group of fighters accustomed to playing dirty. Not even Hawkshaw would back him.

"Then I must learn to fight like a thief in the night? Like a villain? Is that what you are saying?"

"Did you think war would be an honourable affair?"

"Yes," he snapped back to laughter from Hawkshaw, causing Paget to answer him.

"You, Sir, you came looking to settle a dispute in an honourable fashion with Captain Craven, and so why is this so funny to you?"

"Because I came to settle an affair of honour between two officers, in the same army, no less. You seem to think you will be given the same respect by some stranger who owes you nothing."

Paget looked angry that none of his friends defended him against the newcomer, and so he looked to Charlie for aid.

"What is so objectionable to you about this? You have

killed plenty of men, but this offends you?"

"Knives in the back and wearing the uniform of the enemy as we sneak about in the dark, it is not the work of a gentleman."

Craven could not understand his sudden protest after they had all been through until he realised the one factor that had changed, the arrival of Hawkshaw, a well-spoken and well-off gentleman, which he now used as a yardstick. Craven turned to his newly discovered brother to use him in the argument.

"Captain Hawkshaw, as an officer and gentleman who is more recently arrived from England than any of us here; tell me, what is the correct thing to do in the face of such a threat?"

"A gentleman has a responsibility to himself and those around him, and there is no limit to what must be done to protect himself and others."

"You would lower yourself into the gutter like this?" Paget was shocked at his unexpected response to Craven.

Hawkshaw took off his sword belt and handed it to Benning before taking the two staves from Moxy who had just arrived on deck. He gave one to Paget before standing back and holding the other as a weapon.

"We may not always like the way war is conducted, but we must conduct ourselves in it, nonetheless. And I should not forgo such knowledge because of my pride, only to come undone by it by some brigand in the dark of night."

He held out the stave as though it were a sword, extending it from his body with his left hand floating in the air as though he was to fence with foil. Joze went forward and took the stave from Paget who provided little resistance, not wanting to be there at all. Hawkshaw saluted him to begin.

The young street-smart Portuguese man held the stave

close to his body and leaned forward, extending his left hand forward as well. Hawkshaw began to circle him, but Joze leapt forward and pushed his stick out of the way, presenting his own to Hawkshaw's stomach. He then pretended to stab him multiple times. Hawkshaw looked stunned.

"A knife fight is nothing like a sword duel," announced Craven.

"Yes, I am starting to see that," replied Hawkshaw as Paget smiled at his defeat and started to get into the spirit of things.

"You don't learn to fight with a knife from a gentleman or a scholar or even a dancer. Look at what the most practical and dirtiest fighters do, and you will have your answer. You see what Joze did. He hid his weapon from you and controlled yours with his offhand. Think of your left hand like a shield, defending and controlling until the time is right for you to strike with your right. Birback!"

The Scotsman stepped forward.

"Give him the stave," Craven ordered Hawkshaw.

Birback took the wooden stave and put it into a reverse grip, pointing down like a pick before tucking it close to his body.

"How do you win a knife fight, Birback?"

"With violence!" He then leapt towards Joze, smashing his left hand down with his own, knocking his other hand as it came forward with the stave so hard the lighter man was turned around. Birback was on him in seconds, dropping the point of his stave down onto the Portuguese man's neck.

Joze smiled in amazement as he stamped on Birback's foot and dropped low. He grabbed hold of Birback's leg and pushed all his weight forward, causing him to topple over. He crashed to the deck where Joze pinned his weapon down and pretended to stab him in the chest. Birback smiled gleefully as he got back to his feet.

"Well, Paget, do you want to fight dirty or die gracefully?" Craven asked.

He looked to Charlie, finding no sympathy with her at all as he went to Joze and snatched the stave from his hands. Birback got to his feet for a fresh contest, despite his hard landing on the deck just moments before.

"Begin!" Craven roared.

Paget rushed forward and ducked under Birback's big paw, which reached out to smother him. As the Scotsman's pick gripped stave came for him, he beat it aside, leaping up to drive his knee into Birback's stomach. It caused the wind to be taken from him as he gasped, and his eyes popped wide open in shock. His stave fell from his hands as he toppled to his knees. Paget towered over the man that was twice his size and held his stave to Birback's neck as if to slit his throat.

"I didn't say I can't fight dirty. I just don't like to," snarled Paget.

Payne giggled at the display and began to cackle with joy, as Paget struggled to help the much heavier Birback back to his feet.

"A curious body of men you have collected," declared Hawkshaw to Craven.

"Collected suggests any of them were my choice. No, these fine fellows somehow found me, just like you did," smiled Craven.

"Are we done here, Sir?" Paget demanded.

"We surely are," replied Craven being most pleased with the display, and yet Paget stormed off seemingly in anger, causing Charlie to follow him.

"What is it?" The two of them leaned over the deck near the bow of the ship, "Is this about Hawkshaw?"

But he shook his head.

"Then what? What is wrong?"

"I came to fight in Portugal and Spain, and hopefully France one day, but we now sail thousands of miles from where we are needed. That is what's wrong."

"It is not Craven who had you come out here, remember that."

"I know," sighed Paget.

"It will be many weeks yet before the army can move, and we will be back in time for when that happens," added Charlie as she tried to console him.

"It's just we have waited so many months for our chance at the French, and now it has been snatched from us."

"If the intelligence we have about Cairo is correct, we will find Frenchmen here, too, more than we will find waiting at the lines of Lisbon, and have you not always wanted to see Egypt?"

Paget smiled as he was reminded of the dreams of his childhood, which had ended the moment he arrived in Portugal and met Craven.

"I very much would, but not like this. I would have us see the great sights of antiquity, not toil in the mud with the most wretched of backstabbers."

"Are you referring to us or the Egyptians?"

"My understanding is Cairo is under the rule of the Turks in these days," he replied in a scholarly fashion.

"You know what I mean," snapped Charlie.

"Fighting without a uniform feels wrong. I could somehow justify it whilst we were still in Portugal, but out here far from the army and a country's people who want us there, it feels wrong," he replied, looking down at his drab civilian clothes with disgust.

"Think of Major Thornhill."

"How so?" he asked curiously.

"All of the intelligence he supplies Wellington and us, this is the kind of way he discovers it, with missions like this, with the kind of tasks which are never written about in the newspapers."

"That is the problem."

"You care that much about fame?"

"No, that the reason such tasks are not reported. It is because they are shameful."

"That is not how they will be remembered."

"No?" Paget's demeanour became even angrier.

"Not once we have won this war. Such deeds will be written about as heroic endeavours conducted by fearless adventurers."

"You really believe that?"

"I know it, and if you don't believe me, go and ask Captain Payne about the war in America. They celebrate their spies and agents of their war of independence."

"I don't think those traitors are a measure by which we would like to be judged."

"And yet look at them now. Their own proud nation, and one with which England has a fine relation with."

Paget groaned in acceptance.

"You want to fight a war the way of a folk hero, or like something out of the great myths of the Greeks?"

"Yes, yes I would."

"But you know that is not real, and behind every one of those stories, the real truth looks more like this. Great heroic deeds are remembered, but it is here where they are built in work such as this."

Paget thought on it for a while before nodding in agreement but also surprise.

"Where did you learn such reason?"

"On the road with an army," she smiled.

CHAPTER 11

"Land! Land!" a hoarse voice called out.

Paget hurried to the man's side to see for himself. The rest of his comrades rushed up from below deck, more excited for the relief of dry land than the excitement of seeing the hallowed ground of an ancient enigma, the mysterious ancestor to the intellectual world as he saw it, and a great many others, too. The anticipation and excitement caused all his fears to quickly fade away, and it was not long before they were dropping anchor, but the sun was also already low in the sky.

"Is that it? Cairo?" Craven asked.

"Alexandria. Cairo is a few days' ride from here," replied Payne.

"Then we should get ashore quickly and be on our way."

Paget agreed, as he was eager to step foot in the exotic land, but Payne was already shaking his head.

"No, soon it will be dark, and it would be foolish to go

ashore. You will not find any assistance at this time, and there is little light at night."

Craven sighed at the prospect of another night at sea, despite the land being almost close enough he could touch it. But the night drew in remarkably quickly, just as the ship's Captain said it would. The city was swallowed by the night so that one could imagine they were a hundred leagues from land if they hadn't seen it with their own eyes that day.

"We should get some rest. For we will need our strength tomorrow," insisted Matthys. He eventually went below deck, but Craven and Paget were restless and remained up top for very different reasons. Paget for the anticipation of what he might witness in a land he had always dreamed of seeing. Craven, because he merely yearned for solid ground beneath his feet.

"Do you think it will be worth it, Sir, coming all this way?"

"That rather depends on what we find, if anything."

"Surely something, Sir? That must be so?"

"I am sure we will indeed find something, but I am just not sure it will be related to the war effort."

"But you believe we will encounter trouble, Sir?"

"We are foreigners in a land we know nothing about, and we have plenty worth taking."

"You think we will be robbed for our weapons?"

"People who carry these many weapons have a lot to protect, or that is how anyone but a fool would see it, and in our case they would be right."

"Sir?" Paget asked curiously.

Craven pulled out the heavy purse given him by Major Thornhill.

"Enough coin to buy and procure anything we might

need, from weapons to transport, bribes, anything which might be needing to ensure we progress with the utmost haste."

"I wouldn't let Birback in on that fact, for the temptation to take such a purse may be too much," smiled Paget.

"He's not the only one. A year or two ago I would have been the first to elope with such a bag of treasure. I'd already be in the Americas by now, and likely as poor as before I ever found it," laughed Craven.

"But not now, Sir?"

"We left people behind in Portugal, didn't we? And in Spain, too. You are not the only one to be put out by leaving the front."

"And if you could know for certain Major Bouchard was indeed out here and that is who we were pursuing?"

Craven shook his head. "It wouldn't matter. The time will come for the Major and I to cross paths once more. There is no need to force that scenario."

"It surprises me to hear it, Sir, after the great lengths you went to in pursuit of that man."

"I was chasing my own pride, nothing more. Bouchard scored one over me and now we are equal. If there is to be a third match, then so be it, and if he lives, there surely will be. The world is not large enough for men like him and me. We'll certainly meet again."

Fatigue eventually set in, and Craven fell asleep on the gangway. And yet he seemed to almost spring back awake to find it was first light as the crew hurried about its business. He was sore from sleeping on the hard deck, and his body creaked as he got up, and yet he at least felt somewhat rested.

"So eager to get out there you did not even reach your

bed?" Hawkshaw asked who looked significantly more rested and fresher.

"If there was a real bed to have, I would have found it."

Craven looked out to the city where he found a yellow mist extended out across the entire coastline, giving little insight into what lay ahead for them as it was well concealed by the veil of vapours. The ship's boat was already being lowered into the water, and finally, Craven could see his hopes of standing on firm ground were now in sight. The fact that many on that ground would want to rob or kill him was of no consequence at all, not after the dangers they had faced in Portugal. Captain Payne leaned over the quarterdeck as he watched the men work, content to rest on his laurels.

"You will be here when we return?" Craven shouted to him from the gangway below.

"I have been paid most handsomely to wait on your return, Captain, and for every day we wait, we will be paid more."

"Then you have little motivation to see us return at all?" Paget asked.

"If only that were true, for most of our payment will be delivered upon your safe return to Lisbon."

"Then you would do well to see no harm comes to us. I am surprised you do not come along to protect your investment," declared Craven.

"I will risk wasting my time for what I might be paid, but not my life. That is a soldier's job," smiled Payne.

"And if we never return? What then?"

"Then I shall call this a holiday and enjoy the bars and bistros of the city before sailing on to the next work."

"How long will you wait?"

"You've got twenty days."

"And that will be enough?" Paget asked in surprise.

"This mission is barely a wild stab in the dark. Maybe we find something, maybe we find nothing," replied Craven.

"Remember, you have no friends here, so do not look for trouble."

"Isn't that what we came looking for?" Birback grinned.

Craven nodded in agreement before leading the way overboard. They climbed down a cargo net which had been slung over the side of the hull to use as a broad ladder. Only three of the ship's crew waited in the heavy boat, though it would be enough to travel back to the Margaretta across the calm waters. They were soon on their way as several of Craven's comrades took up oars so they may get to the haven they were aiming for. As they closed the distance and could see more through the fog, the mysterious and curious lands lay beyond. The city extended up to the shoreline with densely packed sand-coloured buildings in fantastically square geometry. It was entirely alien to all their eyes, except for Caffy, who did not even blink at the sight. Natural havens stretched out into the sea where fishing boats and transports came and went. It was a bustling city, but there were also many collapsed buildings lying in rubble. They were not ancient ruins but evidence of more recent damage.

"Must have been quite a fight here," said Moxy as he studied it carefully.

"Napoleon took it not many years ago, and our troops laid siege here for many months before the French surrender," replied Paget.

"That was before my time. I was but a schoolboy when I remember hearing such news, and the death of Sir Abercrombie from his wounds suffered in the early days of it. Why would Napoleon come looking for troops all the way out here?" Hawkshaw asked.

"Rumour has it he amasses troops in France for an operation elsewhere. Perhaps he does intend to try for England once more?" replied Matthys.

"He could never do it, not whilst the Royal Navy rules the waves." Hawkshaw, along with his associate Benning, were the only amongst them who had travelled the English Channel in the last year and seen the situation for themselves.

"Across the mainland, then? Is there anywhere he cannot reach?" Paget asked.

"Be thankful of that ambition, for I would not have him come back to Spain, for the last time was enough," replied Craven.

"You would not want to face Napoleon, Sir? I am surprised."

"Not yet, we have barely survived the year of 1810 and now face great enough threats. I fear if Napoleon were to come South, it would all be over."

"You do not believe Wellington could beat him?" Hawkshaw asked in astonishment.

"With an army of equal strength, yes, but Napoleon could march a million soldiers down to Lisbon and sweep Wellington away like he was nothing."

"And so you think the French armies in Spain now look to gather more troops to their side so they may gain victory whilst Napoleon is left free to conduct another war? Is that not madness?"

"It is ambition, of which Napoleon is made of," replied Paget.

They rowed on, and it was not long before they got their first view of the Turks, which for most of them was the first encounter they had with such people, but it was hard to not think of Amyn as they looked upon the large beards and flowing clothes. Hard taskmasters yelled at their slaves as they oversaw much of the work. Though it was not a peculiar sight to those who served in the British Army and often felt they were treated much the same.

They rowed past a natural harbour and leapt from the boat, rushing out of ankle-deep water and onto the beach. They were quickly swarmed by local drivers of primitive donkey drawn carriages just like the hackney carriages seen throughout London. Not one of them spoke a word of English or French, as Hawkshaw quickly found out upon trying both.

"What do we do, Sir?" Paget asked in a confused state as the drivers continued to harangue them for trade.

He looked out all around them for some idea when he noticed a line of five horses being led along a street. He pointed one of the donkey drivers towards them.

"Horses!" He held up the large coin purse given him by Major Thornhill and rattled it in the poor fellow's face. His eyes lit up as he suddenly grabbed at the bag Craven carried and ripped it from his grasp, tossing it into one of the carts. He gestured for Craven to join him.

It was a manic scene on the edge of the bustling city as hundreds of men vied for trade from travellers. Others exchanged coin and commodities, and all the while the slave drivers cried out, seemingly not in an angry fashion, but an affirming one as if it were just any other day. The rest of the group mounted up over several more carts behind Craven's. Paget leapt up beside him, and they all did the best they could to communicate what they wanted. Yet the drivers appeared very certain they already knew what was wanted, despite not understanding a word. In just a few brief moments they were off and being carted along the streets of the city.

Now closer to the damage caused by the siege, they could see work was well underway to make repairs. It was a busy and bustling city that Paget looked upon like a child seeing everything for the first time.

"Keep an eye and a hand on everything you have," ordered Craven as he looked around at every one of the locals with suspicion, as if expecting one of them to try and attack or steal from them in any moment.

"They are just going about their lives, the same as the rest of us," replied Paget.

"Your bag."

"What?" Paget looked around. The satchel he had brought was gone from his side. Across the street he saw it vanishing off into the crowd tucked under the arm of one such local.

"Stop!" Paget moved to jump from the moving cart, but Craven held him firmly in place.

"Whatever you just lost can be replaced. Let us keep an eye on the task at hand."

Paget sighed in frustration but had learned his lesson. His left hand took firm hold of his sword hilt, and he watched all around them like a fox. Craven could see how rattled he was.

"What did you lose?" he asked more sympathetically.

"Nothing of personal value, but items of great need. A blanket, water canteen, and socks."

"Socks?"

"I would never be anywhere without spare socks. It is a great lesson in life I have never forgotten."

"Then we must find you new ones with most haste," jabbed Craven playfully.

"You joke, but there are some things in life which one cannot do without, the bare necessities."

"The clothes on ones back and a sword in hand, I find are enough to ensure one always has what they need."

For almost half an hour they travelled through the most irregular of torturous narrow streets. Almost every home had projecting fronts extending ever further into the streets with each successive floor, as to nearly blot out the sky and daylight above them.

Finally, they passed through a tight gatehouse and into the inner courtyard of one of the largest buildings they had seen yet. They were drawn to a standstill. There were balconies on all sides of the courtyard with steps leading to them. A few men were leaning over one wall smoking pipes in conversation. Craven's driver held out his hand to demand payment, and Craven took out some coins and handed them to him. He knew it would be more than he needed to pay, and yet the man took it and waited for them to leave.

Paget leapt off enthusiastically, eagerly awaiting the next new experience as if it were all some great adventure. In the blink of an eye their few bags had been tossed off into the courtyard, and the donkey drawn carriages were again on their way as they hurried to find more customers. As Craven looked up to two men smoking, he realised there may have been another reason for the driver's sharp exit.

"Where have they taken us, Sir? I see no horses nor horse trader here."

But his curiosity was quickly diminished as he could see Craven's suspicious glance and subtle reach towards the grip of his sword. He looked back and could see the two men glaring back at them, which is when Paget realised they were not locals. For despite some tan to their skin, they looked remarkably more familiar than anyone they had seen since arriving in this new land.

"Did we just pay to be delivered straight to the enemy?" Hawkshaw had noticed their concerns as he studied their surroundings for himself. He heard the click of the lock of Moxy's American rifle as it was slowly and quietly made ready to fire as they formed a circle back-to-back just as the balconies began to fill up with other men. They were all armed with a mixture of carbines and swords, but none were aimed directly at them. It was as if they thought the threat of their presence would be enough to force a surrender. Within a few moments, there were thirty armed men on the balconies and doorways below, and three more men stepped out across the single entrance from where they had arrived to block their exit. None of them wore uniforms, but their trousers, boots, and weapons gave their identity away immediately, for it was not so well concealed. They were French soldiers in civilian jackets and hats.

"They must have paid the locals to deliver anyone suspected of being English soldiers right to them," muttered Matthys.

Finally, a uniformed French officer stepped out onto one

of the balconies as he put on his hat and stepped into view. For a moment Craven's heart raced as he imagined it might be Major Bouchard, but as the man raised his head, he was not recognised by any of them.

"What is your name and rank?" he demanded, looking to identify who was in charge.

"They don't know who you are," Matthys whispered to Craven.

"They will if we let any of them live," replied Hawkshaw.

"I think you overestimate our odds."

"What do we do, Sir?" Paget asked.

"The only thing we can do, we fight our way through," he replied calmly before the officer went on as he carefully studied the enemy.

"You are ordered to surrender your weapons!" the Frenchman shouted.

"This is not Portugal or Spain, nor France or England, we need not fight here!" Hawkshaw roared after being frustrated at Craven's silence, but he soon drew the gaze of the French officer. As a result, he gestured towards one of his sergeants who approached the party, heading for Hawkshaw as he drew out a short sabre.

"We have to do something, now," demanded Birback.

A shot rang out at the entrance drawing all of their attention, only to see the carbine had fired into the air as its wielder had his throat slit. His two comrades already lay dead, and Amyn rushed into the courtyard. He tossed his knife at the sergeant who advanced towards Hawkshaw, embedding it in his chest. He then drew out a brace of fine gilt barrel pistols and shot down two more of the Frenchmen. It took a few moments for the men on both sides to snap out of the show of what they were seeing. Amyn already had his gleaming kilij blade in hand and was upon another of the soldiers as he hurried to cock his carbine. He was cut down as he fumbled it.

Craven ripped his sword from its scabbard just as he saw figures rise up from the rooftops above. They were dressed as Amyn was and fired onto the Frenchmen on the balconies, causing some to try to return fire whilst others ducked for cover. The French officer looked stunned as he leaned over the balcony for a better look, only to have his hat shot off from his head as a musket ball grazed his head. He staggered back in shock and went for cover inside the room he had first come from. Another four swordsmen rushed through the open doorway, following on after Amyn and setting about the Frenchmen with ruthless vigour.

The rest of the French troops hurried in a panic to defend themselves, thrown completely off guard; having thought they had set a perfect trap only to be ensnared in one themselves. Birback had a tomahawk in each hand now as he spun around and looked at the chaos with glee. His eyes glazed over with excitement before he let out a warbling war cry and ran towards the nearest enemies. He threw his axe into the head of one and jumped onto another as he attempted to draw his sword.

Craven rushed for the steps leading to the balcony where the enemy officer had retreated but was met by a tall man with a large sabre. Craven was in no mood for a drawn-out contest, and as a powerful cut was levelled at his head, he lifted his hilt high to his left, letting the blade hang low so the big man's sword glanced off of his own. He spun it around in a manoeuvre more familiar to the cavalry as his German blade rotated rapidly. It cut down hard into the Frenchman's neck and dropped him in one.

Gunfire and the clash of cold steel echoed out about the courtyard as a battle ensued. He stopped at the top of the steps to check on their progress. Everywhere he looked the enemy troops who thought to capture them were now furiously engaged in a deadly battle with his comrades and those of Amyn's countrymen.

Hawkshaw hurried up the steps to follow him with a blood-soaked blade in hand. They both rushed to the doorway to look for the French leader but found themselves looking down the barrel of a large bore pistol. Craven threw out his arm and shoved Hawkshaw back, swinging them both clear of the doorway as the powder in the pan flashed. Fire surged from the barrel so closely, they could feel it warm their faces as the shot blasted past them.

Hawkshaw looked stunned, as much for having come close to death, as the fact it was Craven who saved him without a second of doubt. He could not move as he came to terms with it, and Craven rushed in through the door. The officer held out his sword, but Craven smashed it down with a single callous blow and no respect for his adversary's skills at all. It left him helpless as he held out his empty hands in surrender and began shaking in fear.

"Sit down!" Craven shouted, but the man was frozen in fear. Craven grabbed hold of his tunic and threw him down into a chair.

"Who is your commanding officer? Who set you in place here?"

When he did not get an answer, he slapped the officer across the face, not so hard as to do serious harm, but in an attempt to get a response.

"Captain, this man is an officer!" Hawkshaw came into the room and witnessed the violent display.

Craven let go of the Frenchman with a sigh.

"An officer who did not show us such respect."

"Do we look like officers? We do not even wear a uniform, but he does."

The gunfire and clash of steel was beginning to come to end outside. Craven sighed with frustration, and Hawkshaw began to talk in French to the captured officer. He replied, but seemingly stunned and horrified by how he was being treated. Craven had seen enough. He shoved Hawkshaw aside and took hold of the Frenchman once more.

"Who are you working for?" he demanded, and when he did not get a response, he punched the man in the face, far more unkindly than the slap he had given him before. The man winced in pain as blood trickled from his nostrils, and Craven primed his hand for another strike.

"Captain Craven!" Hawkshaw cried out.

He stopped, but only because he saw the Frenchman's eyes widen and his expression turned from fear to shock.

"Yes, Craven, you know that name, don't you? And you know what I am saying, don't you?" He shook the officer angrily, but he began to laugh in response.

"What? What is so funny?"

The Frenchman finally replied to him, his tone completely changed, and his cocky arrogance had returned.

Craven's anger turned to amusement as he realised what was happening.

"Yes, you heard that name, Craven, and you know exactly

what we're saying, don't you? You frog bastard," smirked Craven.

The Frenchman smiled in response as his cowering act slipped away and a confident and strong man took its place.

"We had expected someone of note to fall into our trap, but never Captain Craven himself," he chuckled.

"Except I have not fallen into your trap, have I!" Craven roared triumphantly as he let the Frenchman go and paced back across the room.

"What now?" Hawkshaw asked.

Craven shook his head as he looked out of the doorway where they had almost met their end. He turned back just in time to see the officer draw out a knife from his boot and rise up towards him. He reacted out of instinct and took hold of the man's wrist below the weapon. With his other hand, he wrapped his hand around the man's hand, encasing the weapon as his knuckles crunched from the grip. Craven drove it into his chest before he had time to think about what he had done. He let go as the man staggered back and slumped into the chair, blood gushing from his mouth as he reached for the knife.

"No!" Hawkshaw cried.

But the officer drew out the weapon, causing a stream of blood to follow, and he had only enough time to smile at his final victory over them before slumping down dead.

"What have you done?"

"He came at me!" Craven snapped.

"I don't care that you killed him, but he was the only hope we had of discovering what the French are doing here! Didn't you see that?"

Craven breathed a sigh of relief, remembering how close

they had come to capture.

"We must count ourselves lucky, for this mission was almost over before it had even got started." He went out to the balcony and looked out of the courtyard. The remaining Frenchmen were lined up as prisoners.

"It seems you have an angel looking out for you, but he is not like any I would have imagined." Hawkshaw leaned out over the balcony beside Craven as he looked down at the Mamluk swordsman cleaning the blood from his blade.

CHAPTER 12

Craven sat down on a large barrel and looked at the devastation around them, imagining how close they had come to disaster. Amyn approached calmly as if he had planned it all along.

"How did you know? How could you have known of any of this, and been ready and willing to mount such an operation?"

"My people watch any foreign soldiers who come to my country with great suspicion. They arrived a little over a week ago and were most generous with coin to anyone who would ensure any Englishmen who arrived were brought to them."

"But why would you intervene?"

"I would not, but I received a message from your Major Thornhill two nights past, and so I knew you would be amongst these Englishmen."

"But you paid your debt to me. You owed me nothing."

"True, and yet the Major sent monies which were most enticing, and with the promise of more to come should I ensure your safety."

Craven smiled, as he finally understood.

"And them? What will we do with them?" Craven looked to the line of prisoners they had taken. Paget and Hawkshaw had already grilled them for information as Matthys oversaw them. But they soon all gave up in frustration and joined Craven.

"They will not give anything up," declared Hawkshaw.

"Because they likely know nothing."

"And you killed the only man who did."

"And them?" Matthys looked across to the survivors.

Amyn yelled at some of his troops who quickly formed up an impromptu firing squad.

"What are you doing?" Paget demanded.

"This is not our business," replied Craven.

"Stop them!" Paget cried out at Amyn, who calmly got to his feet and looked down at Paget with fury.

"Those men fight under the uniform of France, and the same leader who came to my country and took it with a vast army. My people are not quick to forget the great battle at the Pyramids, a shameful defeat," he growled before pointing for his men to go on. Musket fire rang out, and the executions were quickly completed before Paget could get in another word. He looked to Matthys for help, knowing he would not find any empathy amongst the others, but not even the Sergeant would back him, and so he took his protests to Craven.

"Captain, this savagery cannot be allowed!"

"What would you have done with them? We have no means of taking prisoners and this is not our country, nor have we been invited here. We are nothing more than travellers who would do well to travel as quietly as possible."

"And you call this quiet?"

"It was them or us," replied Charlie.

"Yes, when they were armed, but not that!" he cried out, pointing to the unarmed men who had been executed, and yet he looked in amazement that nobody seemed to care.

"Does nobody care?" he asked hopelessly.

Craven got back to his feet with a sigh.

"I don't care about what I cannot change. We didn't come here to fight. We came to hunt. You know that."

"And this is what we are now?"

"We are what we must be. If that troubles you, then go back to the Margaretta and wait for our return," replied Craven unsympathetically.

"You know I cannot do that, Sir."

"Then let's move forward." He turned back to Amyn.

"Thank you, but I must ask for further assistance. You have information on the Frenchmen who have come here, or you would never have known of this place. What else can you tell us?"

"I do not know much about their meaning, but the Ottoman governor Muhammad Ali Pasha has called a great gathering in Cairo."

"And you think the French presence here is related?"

"He welcomes the Mamluks into the city, and it must only be as a gesture of peace, or to gather forces for war."

"Will you go?"

"I must, it is my duty," insisted Amyn.

"When?"

"Five days from now."

"There must be something else we can do before then?"

Paget asked.

"Tell me what you are looking for, and I will help you to find it."

Paget looked to the others for help, as he wasn't even sure.

"We seek out any Frenchmen who have arrived here in the last month," declared Craven.

"If there are more besides those who lie dead around you, then I do not know of them."

"Then what do we do?" Hawkshaw asked.

"What of this mess?" Craven looked around at the bodies and bloodshed.

"There is much of worth here and many men who would see to the work for it. It will not be a problem."

"Nobody is going to draw issue with a few dozen dead men?" Paget asked in horror.

"Nobody here will care for them," replied Amyn calmly.

"Then what now?" Craven asked.

"I can provide you with shelter and comforts nearby or provide horses so that you may go ahead to Cairo."

"Thank you, if we may take the horses, we must go on and see what we can find."

"Without a guide? Sir, I must protest!" Paget interrupted.

"Take Solak with you. He speaks only a little of your language, but enough to be of assistance." Amyn pointed to one of the fighters nearby. He was of a scrawny build with an emaciated looking face, which was much wilted by far too many hours in the sun. Yet nobody doubted his ability as he wiped blood from the blade he had so recently used with such skill.

"Be careful in Cairo. Many forces struggle for power, and nobody is safe."

"Thank you, Amyn, truly."

"A man will do much for a bag of coin," admitted Amyn, and yet Craven could see there was more to it as their friendship had been cemented in battle.

"Come," Solak demanded as he led them out of the courtyard.

Amyn's men stripped the French prisoners bare of anything with any value. They were led to an open yard nearby where several men waited with two-dozen horses. Solak barked his orders to the men who removed weapons from the saddles before handing the animals over to Craven and the others.

"What is your name?" Paget asked curiously as he took one of the horses. It was a small mount but well suited to his frame, and he could see the animal was fit and strong, despite a long-healed scar on its back. It could only have been delivered by a sword blade. Paget ran his hand over the beast's withers and down to its shoulder as he calmed the animal and became accustomed to it.

"This animal has lived a hard life but has only become harder for it."

"Like everything else in this country, it seems," admitted Hawkshaw.

Solak led them on without a single word as they passed through the city, gazed upon with suspicion as they were before, but no longer toyed with. Their guide rode through the crowds like a king. The people soon got out of his way, and he whipped several who did not. It seemed to take an age to battle their way out of the congested city that was far larger than any of them had imagined, with hundreds if not thousands of people lining every street. But eventually, they were clear of it and on the road

South to Cairo, along with a great many more travellers and traders. It was a bleak land, and yet the scope and scale of the vast plains used only for agriculture.

"I imagined so much more," said Paget as he rode beside Craven,

"This country has not been the great empire you read about in books for thousands of years."

"There is still some beauty to it, but I had expected great dunes of sand and sculptures."

"You will have much to marvel at when we reach Cairo." Hawkshaw drew up beside them.

"You have visited?" Paget asked excitedly.

"No, but I have been told about it by those who have. They say no work of art can truly capture the magnificence of the Pyramids, a great wonder of the ancient world, which I have longed to see. I must admit I never imagined it would be under such circumstances, though."

"Enjoy it whilst you can but remember how hostile a place this can be. The French may not be the only ones who want us dead, for we are nothing to these people. We wear no uniforms, and we are no more than travellers who would not be missed by anyone."

"Not even by Wellington, Sir?"

"Even if we were to never return, what would the army do? What could Wellington do? Do you think he would land an army here in search of us?"

Paget looked dumbfounded and yet shook his head in acknowledgement.

"If the French can make some treaty here, we may be in even greater danger," added Hawkshaw.

"Yes, so we must tread lightly."

"Can you do that, Sir?" Paget asked, causing Hawkshaw to laugh in amusement.

It was an uneventful ride for several days, but the anticipation of what they would see at the end of it was enough to keep Paget fired up. On the third day they stopped as he gasped at the first glimpse of them. Far into the distance they could see the great monoliths towering over the city of Giza before them in a magnificent fog. It gave them a magical appearance as the ancient city stretched out to Cairo, so they were barely indistinguishable from one another.

"This is it. This is what I had imagined my life to be if it had not been in service of the King."

"Then feel yourself doubly lucky, as the King paid for your travel," smiled Craven.

"Magnificent, to behold something so ancient just as it as back then."

But their guide led them on, for it was nothing of note to him.

"Come on, I would be in the city and with lodgings before nightfall," insisted Craven after days on the road. Paget followed on but could not take his gaze from the vast monuments ahead as he looked upon them in awe.

"They are quite something, aren't they?" Charlie admitted as she rode beside him.

"I have wanted to see them from the moment I knew of their existence as a young boy. I had long given up hope of ever beholding them, but now we are really here, I cannot believe it."

As they approached Cairo, they would see it was a far more magnificent city than Alexandria, but the night was drawing in. Solak arranged accommodations for them in a somewhat lavish establishment compared to what they had experienced in the country so far. Great columns supported the balconies of the building, and they entered to find it was a virtual palace. Their modest luggage and coats were taken from them, and they sat down in a lounge fit for a king as wine and glasses were brought to them.

Solak stopped before Craven and held out his hand. Knowing their lavish lodgings must be paid for, he delved into the purse he had been given and took a handful of coins, holding them out in an open hand to allow Solak to take what he needed. Astonishingly, he took only a few before handing them to a frontman at the hotel.

"Money goes a long way here," smiled Hawkshaw as one of the hotel staff poured a glass of wine for him. He took a sip and slumped down into a large armchair. Birback's face lit up at the decadence all around them, as he downed a glass of wine, and held it out to be refilled in a somewhat novel experience.

"Well, this I could get used to!" he roared as he slumped down and extended his boots out onto a table, making himself most comfortable without any care for manners.

"Now what? What will we do here?" Hawkshaw asked.

"In the morning we will continue our search for the Frenchmen who came here, but tonight we drink," smiled Craven as he took up a glass.

"To victory in Portugal!"

Paget held up one himself.

* * *

The morning sun and heat caused Craven to stir, and he awoke in a lavish room and a soft bed. He sat up and pulled on his boots as he went to a balcony overlooking the street below. It was warm but not excessive, as it felt like a comfortable summer's day back in England, and a welcome retreat from the bitter winds and rain in Portugal. The streets were already filling up with people as they went about their business, but it was clear they were in a wealthy part of the city, as most were empty-handed and not going about hard chores.

"Captain Craven!"

He leaned over the balcony to see Lieutenant Paget eagerly waving to him from below. Craven shook his head angrily, but Paget couldn't understand why as Craven grabbed his long coat and headed for the stairs to join the young man and chastise him.

"Do not use my rank, nor that name either," he growled.

"But what should I call you, Sir?"

"Not, sir, that's for certain," snapped Craven,

He sighed as he looked around to be sure nobody was watching them, conscious of the fact his name had just been hurled out for all to hear.

"Walker, call me John Walker."

"Sir, I mean Walker…"

"John," replied Craven as he tried to be as subtle as possible.

"Solak says there are some Frenchmen who are currently in the city, several groups of them in fact."

"What else?"

"I am afraid his grasp of English doesn't allow much more

explanation, and it took some time to extract that out of him. I fear he is a man of few words even in his own tongue."

Matthys and Hawkshaw stepped out to join them as they planned their next steps in a very alien environment.

"It will be a tall order finding anything in this city," declared Hawkshaw.

"We have navigated Portugal, Sir, so I think we can manage here."

Craven scowled at Paget once more for his address but needed not say anything, as Paget realised his mistake.

"The difference is the people of Portugal wanted us there, for the most part. The only thing these people want from us is our money, and anything else of value they can take."

"So, what now, John Walker?"

"That is what you will go by?" Hawkshaw smiled at him.

"My name is a danger to us all, and so you will all use this one if you want to live to see England again, or even Portugal for that matter."

"John Walker? I remember him breaking a few skulls," said Matthys as he was reminded of endearing memories.

"It's as good a name as any. Solak says he knows of several groups of Frenchmen. I suggest we let him lead us to them and see what we can find," replied Craven as the rest of them came out from the hotel.

Birback staggered out with his shirt hanging out and his jacket and sword slung under one arm as he drank from a wine bottle. He was barely able to walk in a straight line.

"Did you even sleep?" Matthys asked in disgust.

"Of course, but a little more wine can do no harm," laughed Birback.

"Just because we are not in uniform that is no reason to be a drunken fool," seethed Hawkshaw, just as Benning crashed out onto the street and fell over his own feet. He dropped a wine bottle as he did do and scurried about to retrieve it before he lost all of its contents. He looked even more worse for wear than Birback, leaving Hawkshaw unable to protest any further without looking foolish for his own man being no different.

"Be on your guard," ordered Craven before nodding towards Solak to lead the way.

The city was bleak and sandstone colour in architecture, but with much colour added by the clothing of the inhabitants, as well as canopies and other materials hung in windows and archways. The lavish architecture gave a familiar feel that was almost reminiscent of home for them all, and yet alien at the same time. They were led through busy streets for just a few minutes when they reached another hotel similar to their own. Solak gestured for them to wait, but Craven followed him in anyway and watched as Amyn's man argued with the hotelier. He shared some angry words before walking away.

"French go, gone," declared Solak.

"The men we are looking for will still be here. Their work is not done."

Solak did not understand Paget's words, but he knew exactly what to do. He led them on to the next location as Birback began to protest. He started to sweat as the temperatures began to climb and his hard drinking punished him. They walked on for more than half an hour when finally, they reached an open square.

They could see a group of five Europeans drinking tea around a table. They were unmistakeable, but like Craven and the others, wore no uniform, and yet they had swords on their sides. All of them smallswords, the light and thrust only sword a civilian would commonly wear, but also favoured by many officers, especially in France. Craven stopped as he eyed them up and down. He could hear them speaking French even if he did not understand it.

"What do we do, Sir, I mean, John?"

"We need to know if they are who we are looking for," replied Matthys.

"They are armed Frenchmen, what more do you want to know?" Birback chimed in angrily.

Craven sighed, as he realised they had no plan on how to identify the Frenchmen they were looking for. He turned to Hawkshaw, knowing he was the only one who could communicate with them effectively.

"What?"

"Go and talk with them," ordered Craven.

"To what end? You expect me to ask if they are French spies?"

"You are the French speaker, so go and figure it out."

"Are you actually telling me that the great Captain Craven has no plan for these occasions?"

"Keep your voice down."

Hawkshaw did as he asked as he waited for further orders.

"I'll come with you, but you do the talking. Go fishing and find out what they are doing here."

Hawkshaw sighed before doing as asked, and the two of them wandered over to the Frenchmen. They were dressed in their decadent finery as if the revolution had never come to their country.

"All right, all right," he insisted as he walked over to them with Craven just a few paces behind.

The Frenchmen continued to talk jovially as he stopped and towered over them. Finally, one turned to face him with a disgusted expression of utter contempt. Hawkshaw attempted to initiate a conversation, but the Frenchman merely waited for him to stop speaking before studying Craven also. He then turned his nose up at them and replied in English, clearly recognising that they were not Frenchmen.

"Why are you talking with us? Go away. Go back to England where you belong, or to Spain where you may spill your blood," he replied in a pompous manner.

Hawkshaw looked to Craven for answers now that their cover was blown. Craven pushed him aside to address the Frenchmen personally.

"Your army cannot protect you here, and so why do you not tell us what you are doing here?" he demanded aggressively.

The Frenchman smiled arrogantly in response. "We are enjoying a world we own."

"Funny, because I have seen your countrymen beaten down by Portuguese peasants," goaded Craven.

The Frenchman shot to his feet angrily and took up his drink. He tossed it in Craven's face, but the Captain did not even flinch, as he tasted the liquid, which ran down his face. Suddenly, he snapped a punch into the Frenchman's face, which caused him to cry out as he staggered back and fell over his chair. The rest of his party shot to their feet as he got up, and four more stepped out from a nearby building.

"What have you done?" Hawkshaw demanded.

But the Frenchmen ripped their smallswords from their

scabbards, readying themselves for a fight.

"That's better!" Benning roared as the drunken officer rushed forward and grabbed the chair the Frenchman had fallen over. He threw it at them, striking one and knocking him over before barrelling past and hacking down towards another as a melee ensued.

Paget shook his head in disbelief before going to the aid of Craven and the others. Cold steel clashed, and many of the locals stopped to watch the bizarre display with much curiosity. Benning swung wildly with his sword and was punished by a smallsword thrusting just a small amount into his shoulder. It seemed to anger him more than seriously hurt, as he smiled and went forward against his opponent once more. He cut his smallsword aside and smashed the ward iron of his own sword into his ribs so hard an audible crack rang out as the man folded over in pain.

Paget parried one thrust after another, trying to stop him and others from being harmed whilst making no attempt to hurt the Frenchmen either.

"We have to stop this!" he cried out to Craven.

But the Captain was enjoying himself too much. The tip of a smallsword nicked his hand and caused him to drop his sword, but he rushed to the table the Frenchmen had been sitting at and tipped it over. He broke one of the legs off to use as a weapon and proceeded to beat blades aside and wail on the Frenchmen with his makeshift cudgel. Yet his attention was soon drawn to Paget. The young officer cried out as he was thrust in his arm, having presented no threat and his defences finally failed. He dropped to one knee, and Charlie ran to him as the battle came to a pause. Craven backed away towards Paget, holding out his table leg to keep the Frenchmen at bay.

"Is he okay?" Craven asked Charlie.

"No, I am not okay, I've been stabbed!"

Paget angrily shot to his feet whilst still cradling his wounded arm, leaving his sword on the ground where it had fallen. He stormed toward the Frenchman who had addressed them in English and appeared to be their ringleader. Craven rushed by his side in concern for his protection, but Paget showed no fear as he stopped within thrust range of the man with no weapon of his own.

"Are you here at the request of the French army and Napoleon?"

"What business is it of yours?"

"Our quarrel is with the army of France and those who have invaded those we have alliances with. I repeat, are you here in an official capacity or not?"

"We would have nothing to do with that silly war," replied the Frenchman as if disgusted it would even be implied that they might be.

"And you trust their word?" Hawkshaw asked in disbelief.

"Look at their dress and their swords. These are not soldiers on army business."

Craven shrugged in agreement as they all licked their wounds. Blood had been drawn by several on each side, but all were still standing.

"So this was a misunderstanding?" Hawkshaw asked.

"Yes, and you shall pay for it," snapped the Frenchman, causing all to raise their weapons and ready themselves for a fight once more, except for Paget, and Matthys who rushed to his side to assist.

"Gentlemen, I think enough blood has been spilled here today. Let us not see anymore," he insisted.

"But we did not throw the first blow!"

"Were you not the one to make this matter more than just words? Did you not first cast your drink in an offence quite warranted of a demand of satisfaction?" Matthys asked. The Frenchman looked humbled, knowing it was true and yet frustrated at the same time.

"Be on your way and pray we do not meet again!"

Benning looked eager to go on, and the Frenchman's words infuriated him, but Hawkshaw dragged him away. Craven looked to the wounded Paget and knew he had to rise above his anger. He retrieved his sword and quickly sheathed it before leading them away.

"Was any of that necessary?" Paget asked.

"We needed to know if they were enemy spies, and we now have our answer."

"How so?"

"Because if those were French soldiers or spies, they would have been more interested in fighting or fleeing than maintaining their honour and dignity," he smiled.

Paget shook his head in amazement and yet knew there was method to his madness. The group then stopped to reconsider their next strategy.

"There is still one more place to look," declared Paget.

"Matthys, take Mr Paget back to our accommodations. See to his wounds and any others. The rest are with me," insisted Craven.

"You are hurt, too," insisted Paget.

"That is nothing." Craven shrugged it off, and nobody

dared argue any further. The two groups split up, and Craven's party followed Solak on to the last destination.

"You did not join the fight?" Craven asked him.

"I fight to kill, not play," he replied stoically.

"You're missing out on a lot of fun," smiled Craven as they went on having lost four of their group.

"We would do well to proceed with more caution," Hawkshaw said.

Craven just nodded along as they continued, and Solak led them to a rather rough and secluded part of the city where seemingly no tourist would ever travel. The locals looked them upon with far more suspicion. Eventually, he told them to wait whilst he went into a small establishment tucked away amongst some small residences shared by many families.

"You think this is the kind of place they would find accommodation?" Hawkshaw asked.

"That depends how smart they are and what they are hiding from. It's hard for a European to blend in in these parts, but any other Europeans looking for them wouldn't get much help."

"And which do you think we are pursuing?"

"I think you would send capable men on a task like this. Smart and strong."

But Hawkshaw looked no better informed, as it didn't answer his question at all. Solak soon returned, shaking his head.

"They were not here?"

"Here, but not today."

Craven sighed in frustration.

"This is no good. We don't even know what we are looking for in a city we don't know or understand," he groaned as he kicked a wooden bucket and launched it across the street. It smashed into the wall of someone's home and shattered into many pieces, attracting the attention of several of the locals who looked ready to slip a knife into his back for even being there.

"We should be on our way," insisted Hawkshaw.

Craven huffed with frustration as he led them away empty-handed and no better off than when they had arrived.

CHAPTER 13

Craven paced back and forth angrily on the balcony of his lavish room with Paget and Matthys sitting at a small table inside.

"There is nothing more we can do but wait. The parade tomorrow will surely bring any Frenchmen to the surface," Matthys said.

"Just like Thornhill to throw us out into the unknown with the tiniest sliver of information and no help," growled Craven.

"I thought the Major was most meticulous in his intelligence gathering and planning of operations?" Paget asked.

"When it's his own hide on the line, yes, that's true!"

"This task we were set was always a gamble, and Major Thornhill knew that. There was every chance we wouldn't find anything, and that there was never a French mission to Cairo at all," added Matthys, causing Craven to stamp to a halt as he looked at the two of them expecting more.

"And you, Mr Paget, what do you think?"

"I have always thought everything happens for a reason, Sir, and so we have a purpose here even if it has not yet been revealed to us."

But the sound of horses approaching caused him to rush to the edge of the balcony to see Amyn arriving, which was a welcome sight after their fruitless efforts. He hurried to the stairs to greet the man who he had formed a most unusual bond with. The Mamluk had a huge smile upon his face on arrival, which seemed in stark contrast to the troubled mission Craven had been sent on.

"You bring good news?"

Muhammad Pasha invites us to celebrate the investment of his favourite son, Tusun, with a pelisse of his own and the command of an army."

"An army? To do what?" Paget asked in concern.

"To march against the Wahhabis. We unite against an enemy, and you have been made welcome, along with representatives of the French."

"Why? Why have us both present?" Craven asked.

"To play one against the other and see who is strongest," replied Paget.

"This Pasha, which way does he lean in the war in Europe?"

"Hard to say, for he does not like either you or the French, but where money is involved, alliances may be made," smiled Amyn.

"We do not even wear uniform," admitted Craven as if stunned by the invite to such a significant event.

"You are not welcome as soldiers but as diplomats, and there shall be no blood drawn between you and the French. For it would be unwise to anger Governor Pasha. He can be a ruthless man, and he is more powerful now than ever before."

"And yet he invites your people to this celebration?"

"Yes, all the Beys in Cairo. Many hundreds of Mamluks will gather at the citadel and join in these festivities, and perhaps we shall ride to war together," declared Amyn optimistically. Craven looked to the others, clearly realising how out of his depth he truly was.

"We should go and make a good show of ourselves," replied Hawkshaw.

"We'll go, all right. I just wish we knew what we were getting ourselves into."

"A great celebration the likes of which you have never seen!" Amyn yelled excitedly, "I shall gather you in the morning, sleep well!" he roared with more enthusiasm and excitement than any of them had seen him exhibit before as he rushed away.

Paget's face was lit up with hope of some progress and a marvel to behold, but there was as much concern as there was surprise from most of the others.

"This is some progress at least," admitted Hawkshaw.

Craven looked to Matthys for guidance as he so often did.

"Tomorrow it will be the first day of March. Winter is lifting. Spring is upon our army in Portugal, and so with it the expectation of progress. We should see what comes of the day at least, but if the French cannot gain support here, then we have no part left to play in this land," replied the Sergeant with a calm wisdom.

"And if the French are there tomorrow, what do we do, Sir?" Paget asked.

Craven had to resist the urge to fight as he looked to

Matthys once more, but already knew what he must do.

"We are not here to fight them in this country, only stop them from securing more forces in the war against us."

"And so we oversee this celebration and then merely return to Lisbon?"

He looked to Hawkshaw. "That would be our mission complete."

"And without a fight, well, mostly," added Moxy.

"I would see the Pyramids before our return. It would be a tragedy to have come this close and seen them in the distance with our own eyes but not to experience them."

Craven looked to the others in amazement before bursting into laughter. He was joined by most of the others.

"What is so amusing?"

"That we have a great war to fight. A war to decide the future of all of Europe, perhaps even the whole world, and yet you are set on sightseeing."

"It was not so long ago that you ignored such a calling in pursuit of revenge and a perceived wrongdoing. Is therefore, my desire not more pure?" Paget replied scathingly.

Hawkshaw laughed as he admitted it openly. Night was drawing in, and the wine was soon flowing as they made the most of the evening. Craven looked out pensively across the city.

"It is quite beautiful, is it not?" Matthys leaned against a column beside him.

"In its way, yes, but mostly because this place does not know war, or not as we find it. I have not known a city or even a village not living under the cloud of war since I left England, and even then, people feared the invasion from France. But here, it is peaceful."

"Only to our eyes, who do not know this place, for much war has passed through, and more will come. I would wager if you spoke to the people of this place they would share the same fears, but we do not hear them."

"Do you think we can do it? Return triumphant by doing nothing at all?"

"Perhaps our presence alone is something in itself."

"How do you figure that? I don't understand."

"Our presence shows a willingness to act in these parts. After the war is decided in Europe, no leader here would want the victor of that conflict turning his eye here. Perhaps we are enough to deter any agreement with the French?"

"I surely hope so. With the spring, the wheels of war must be turning, and our work is not here."

But when he got no response, he looked over to see Matthys smiling back at him.

"What?"

"To see you finally found your purpose and your path is something I always dreamed I would see. If I stayed long enough by your side, I hoped you would find your path."

"War is the path you would have me follow?"

"A just war such as this, yes, until the end."

"How did I ever get myself tied up in all this?" Craven smiled at him.

"You were born to fight, and you finally found the right place to do it. Not drunken brawls or bloody displays before a baying rowdy crowd, but here where you can really make a difference."

"Is that what we are doing? Making a difference?" Craven pondered at the suggestion.

"You know that we are, or we would never been allowed to continue on the way we have."

"And what way is that?"

"Your way. The way no leader would ever tolerate, were it not for the results you have achieved."

"Drink!" Benning stumbled onto the scene and handed a glass to each of them, spilling it out over their hands as he did so.

"For people who do not drink, they sure do have a lot of wine on hand," declared Craven.

"Like Amyn said, money is a great motivator," admitted Matthys.

"What do we drink to?" Benning asked.

"To our return to Portugal," replied Craven as he reminisced almost as if it were his home.

The thought of meeting the French the next day weighed heavily on Craven's mind, but the night went quickly as the end of their open-ended mission into the unknown brought great relief. He awoke the next morning fresh, having gone to bed early to make the best of a comfortable bed. Although he found several of the others worse for wear having fallen asleep beside their wine in the lounge downstairs. He kicked Birback's boot as it hung over an armchair. He grunted as he woke up and slumped forward and got to his feet, looking surprisingly alert considering his dishevelled state.

"I could get quite used to this place," he smiled.

But Craven only shook his head at how easily the Scotsman was pleased with a comfortable seat and as much wine as he could drink, only to realise they weren't so different.

"Captain Craven!" Amyn enthusiastically called across to

them.

The sound of his name called aloud grated, especially after having scolded Paget for doing the same. But he could not bear to say anything to their kind host as Craven led the others out into the street. They found Amyn in all of his finery, with the most magnificent of flowing and colourful robes and gold and jewels encrusted about his body. His entourage was almost as decadently attired. Craven looked to his own dirty and well-worn attire and that of his comrades and shrugged.

"I am afraid we are underdressed."

"But you are here!" Amyn roared excitedly as horses were brought for Craven and his party.

They mounted up and followed on. Ever more Mamluks joined them until the procession totalled five hundred of the Mamluk nobles who proudly rode through the city they had once ruled outright. It was a grandiose display, which Paget marvelled at more than any of them as if a dream had come true. It was like nothing any of them had seen before as they paraded as though they were royalty, and crowds cheered at the exotic display.

"Magnificent, is it not, Sir?"

"They parade for war, just like we do."

"And is that not magnificent also?"

"I never really cared for it, but I'll admit this is rather more impressive."

They were led through the narrow winding streets to the great gate of the citadel. It was a magnificent fortress at the heart of the city, which was reminiscent of the great castles and walled cities of England and Wales. Yet whilst most of those lay in ruins, this fortress was bristling with life and in active service.

The tall walls stretched fifty feet up to the sky and had countless towers atop the hill before the first line of walls. A smile did not leave Paget's face the entire time as they rode on as if they were a triumphant army returning home, with all the pomp and fanfare he had dreamed of. As they passed through the great gatehouse, Amyn rode up to join them.

"Only Craven may ride with me as a guest. The others will wait here."

Craven nodded towards them, and whilst they did not like it, nobody argued with the decision, as they knew there was no choice in the matter. Craven took up a position beside Amyn and the Mamluk nobles as an honoured guest, as they rode on up to the centre of the citadel and seat of power in Cairo, and in theory all of Egypt. They came to a broad open courtyard. Around them were tall structures with lavishly domed roofs with the most beautiful of architecture. Several were obviously religious buildings and revered greatly by all around them.

"That is him, the Governor," declared Amyn as they stopped and dismounted.

"Was he once not your enemy?"

"And are you not allied with men who were once your enemy?"

Craven thought of Hawkshaw and remembered how passionately he was pursued by his half-brother and nodded in agreement.

* * *

Paget paced back and forth, eager to know what was going on. He stopped when a unit of Turkish troops moved from a nearby wall on the far side of the inner gatehouse, and he could see a group of Europeans sitting around just as they were.

"There they are," Paget gasped.

The others turned quickly back around to see a familiar face, causing Paget to reach for his sword. Matthys instantly leapt into his path and stopped him taking a step further.

"Bouchard," growled Paget as he tried to go straight at him, but Matthys blocked him, turning to see again for himself and confirm it was the man they suspected.

"No, not here!" Matthys could see the potential for how volatile the situation could be. A hundred Turkish soldiers were guarding the gatehouse, and with no reason to treat them considerately.

"He is right there, healed and ready to put an end to all of this," whispered Paget.

"We are guests here the same as them in this sacred place." Hawkshaw joined them to get a view of the French Major for himself, to see the French Major smiling back at him, raising a cup of coffee in a salute.

"If Craven wanted him so badly, he should have run the bastard through when he had the chance," replied Birback in frustration, as he could still not understand how Craven let the sick Major live.

"Because he is a man of honour," replied Hawkshaw as he came to his brother's aid in an experience that felt most bizarre for all of them.

"What do we do?"

"We do nothing, Moxy, until Craven returns," declared Matthys.

Hawkshaw did not argue with the Sergeant taking control

of the situation. He knew they were all loyal to Craven and would not listen to him anyway. Paget was still pacing back and forth, glaring at Bouchard, and muttering to himself.

"There'll be hell to pay when Craven gets back."

* * *

Craven stepped up before the Governor Pasha and merely bowed a little before moving on, as he seemed to have little care for conversation. Amyn took a cup of coffee from a man carrying a tray full and passed it to him.

"Drink," insisted Amyn.

"I don't understand it. Why are you parading before him when he hates you?"

"We cannot fight every man we dislike, or we may have more enemies than friends."

The pleasantries went on but did not last long before they were mounting their horses once more and riding down the steep and narrow street winding back towards the gates. Craven wondered what it was all for, and yet was reminded of the endless parades of the volunteers, militia, and yeomanry back in England. Ali Pasha's troops proceeded to follow them in a huge snaking parade out of the citadel.

Yet Craven's calm rapidly faded away as he spotted the Frenchmen on one side of the gate ahead of them, and instantly recognised Bouchard. He sat up in the saddle for a closer look before riding out of the formation, causing Amyn to follow him in frustration. Both of them stopped thirty paces short of the French entourage, knowing they could not draw blood as they were guests.

"Captain, we must leave!" Amyn insisted.

But the Mamluk's attention was draw to a commotion ahead. The gatehouse was being closed before them, as many of Pasha's troops climbed into the walls ahead. His face turned to a look of absolute horror as he yelled out to warn his people, but it was too late. Soldiers appeared on the high walls either side of them and at the gatehouse ahead. A volley of musket fire erupted, and a wall of lead struck the unsuspecting Mamluk column. Many fell from the opening salvo, but the enemy were unrelenting, as a second wave rose up from the walls and fired another volley.

Craven looked at the brutal display in amazement and turned back to Bouchard for only a moment. The Major was just as stunned as he. Amyn ripped his sword from its sheath, being the only weapon he had to defend himself with.

"Run!" Craven cried.

Shots continued to rain down on the Mamluks. They were cut down as some tried to climb the walls or beat against doors. Others rushed at the men at the gatehouse with their swords swinging about their heads, in a hopeless attempt to escape or at least die with some glory. Blood and bodies littered the street as hundreds were killed in the first minute. Amyn circled his horse about looking for something he could do, as he felt helpless amid the slaughter.

"Run, or you will die here!" Craven shouted to the man who had saved his life. Amyn didn't need to be told again as he dug in his heels and launched his horse forward.

"Craven!" Paget roared.

Craven looked back to see the slaughter was out of control. Two of the Frenchmen lay dead, and another bloodied one was leaning against Bouchard. Benning had been hit in the arm as his small party took cover but did not fire back, not wanting to anger the murderous Turkish soldiers any further as they continued with their bloody slaughter. A musket ball skimmed the side of Craven's coat arm, and he knew it was time to leave. He galloped back to the gate, just as his comrades reached it, along with Bouchard's men. They shoved several Turkish soldiers out of the way to reach the gate and get it open. The two shared a look of complete disdain and yet equally wanted to get out of there alive.

"Look, Sir!" Paget yelled.

They watched as Amyn directed his horse towards a stone staircase. He crashed through a soldier and galloped up onto the walls, hacking down at another. His horse smashed another man off the top, throwing him to his death. Musket fire still rang out all around as the slaughter continued, with hundreds lying dead, and the last of the Mamluks about to join their fallen.

One soldier tried to grab at Amyn, but he swung back with a wicked backhand strike against the man's face, causing him to fall down dead as he looked around for somewhere to escape. Shots struck the wall beside him, and it was enough to spur him forward. He galloped along the battlements, knocking more of the soldiers aside and hacking down at others until he reached the end of one battlement. There was nowhere left to go as more soldiers rushed after him. He came fifty paces back along the wall, turning around once more as three soldiers backed away, having seen the carnage he had caused. They began to reload their weapons to shoot him from the saddle. Amyn looked down at Craven just briefly with the look of a man who was about to die. He saluted with his sword before spurring his horse on once more and directing the animal to an opening in one of the battlements. He launched out into the open and vanished from sight. Paget could barely believe what he was seeing.

"Come on!" Craven pulled him away, and he caught only one last glimpse of the bloodbath where the last of the Mamluks were being shot down, as the nearly five hundred who had entered lay in a horrific mound of bloody bodies and horses.

Paget passed through the gate to see they had gotten out with only three horses, including the one Craven was atop.

"Where is Bouchard?" he asked, remembering the Turks were far from the only threat.

"He's gone, come on!" Craven led them about the walls, skirting along the citadel rather than away from it. Nobody said it, but they all knew why, for they had all seen the incredible exploits of Amyn. It was not long before they reached the spot where he had jumped and found his horse sprawled out dead across the ground in a gruesome display.

"Where is he? Nobody could have survived that fall," declared Hawkshaw as he looked up at the great height above.

"I fear we have long outstayed our welcome." Matthys looked around with suspicion as if expecting a mob to come after them at any moment.

Craven didn't need to be told twice as the echo of musket fire continued to ring out from the citadel, the ambushing troops making absolutely certain there would be no survivors in a horrifying display of violence.

CHAPTER 14

"What the hell happened back there?" Hawkshaw demanded furiously as Craven took a large glass of wine. The shaken group had gathered in their hotel. Matthys saw to Benning's wound, causing him to wince as he took a bottle from Birback who knew his pain all too well.

"I would say the competition between factions in this country has been settled," replied Paget.

"Settled? We just watched five hundred men be slaughtered at a parade they were welcomed upon as guests!"

"It is not safe for us here any longer. We should be on our way," insisted Matthys as he contemplated their scenario whilst giving aid with a steady hand like the veteran he was.

"But why did they fire on us and the French?" Moxy asked incredulously.

"It wasn't intentional. The slaughter was indiscriminate, and we were in harm's way," replied Craven.

"And what of the rest of the Mamluks across Egypt?" Hawkshaw asked.

"They are to be slaughtered, all of them," came a weary and pained voice from the entrance. It brought them all to silence as they beheld Amyn. His clothing was cut and torn, and he was badly bloodied all over. His bloody sword dangled from his equally bloody hand, its tip resting on the floor, as he was seemingly unable to lift it any longer.

Paget and Hawkshaw rushed to his aid, helping support him until they could lower him down into a chair. Matthys quickly finished his work with Benning to help their battered friend when Craven noticed one of the hotel staff turn to hurry away. He grabbed his arm as he pulled out a knife and placed it upon the man's neck.

"Not a word of this to a soul, do you understand me?"

He wasn't sure if the man would understand his language, but he knew he would get his meaning, as when he nodded, he also trembled. Craven shoved him on.

"Even if that man can be trusted to keep his silence, it will not take long for word to get out, and you rode with the Mamluks. Those murderers will come looking for all of us."

Everyone was silenced by Hawkshaw's words, realising the danger they all faced, as it seemed a whole country was against them.

"The Governor has ordered the slaughter of all the Mamluks," winced Amyn.

"All of them?" Paget was shocked by his words.

"All across the country, he means to eradicate the Mamluks."

"Will he succeed?"

"If he can kill five hundred nobles here in Cairo, then I fear it so, yes."

"We need to leave this place, now!" Craven immediately ordered.

"What about Major Bouchard, Sir?" Paget asked.

"He is in no better a position than us, and he will surely flee back to Spain."

Craven took out the purse given him by Major Thornhill and tossed it to Hawkshaw.

"Take Birback and Joze with you and find us enough horses to depart with immediate haste. I don't care if you have to pay ten times what they are worth or steal them, just get us what we need!"

Hawkshaw looked at the coin bag in a stunned state for a moment, still reeling from the slaughter they had witnessed and the danger they still faced.

"Go! Go now!" Craven shouted.

The three men rushed out to do as ordered as Matthys continued to do his work. The others were too stunned to move, reflecting on the horror they had witnessed.

"This is the end for my people."

"What will you do?" Craven asked.

Amyn shrugged with the look of a man who had lost everything.

"Come with us!" Paget blurted out without even considering his words and what it could mean.

"To what end?"

"What is left for you here?"

Amyn shrugged at Craven's question, as they all knew the answer.

"I can't promise you riches or an easy life."

Amyn smiled, as Craven wasn't really selling it to him.

"But we can promise you that you will be amongst men of honour. Friends," Paget added enthusiastically.

"Why? What have we got that would bind us together?"

Craven paced across the room and picked up the Mamluk's bloody sword.

"This is what we have in common. Fight for us, and we will fight for you just as we once did. Stay here, and you will be hunted for the rest of your life or come with us to Portugal and fight beside us."

"What does it pay?"

"Almost nothing," smiled Craven.

He looked about the room and could see they were all in agreement with Craven's offer. For they had all seen him fight with such ferocity, and his escape from the citadel was enough to impress Benning.

"And your Wellington, what we will he say of it?"

"Wellington needs men who will fight, can you do that?"

Amyn nodded in agreement.

"Then join us and begin anew as most of us have. We have found purpose in Portugal, and you can, too."

Amyn grimaced as Matthys continued to bind his wounds, but the Sergeant also nodded in appreciation towards Craven for the olive branch he was offering, of which he much approved.

"Pasha's soldiers will slaughter us all if we spend another night in this city. We should ride whilst we still have a chance of escaping them."

"But are you able to, Amyn?" Paget asked.

"There isn't any choice, we ride or die," replied Craven as

they heard horses gallop up to the entrance. Craven leaned out to see Hawkshaw and the two others he had sent having returned with all they needed. He had a bloodied nose but tossed the coin purse back to Craven, who noted it was as heavy as when he had sent it away.

"You can keep that," smiled Hawkshaw.

"Is anyone coming for those horses?"

"Probably," Joze said as the three men stayed in their saddles, showing the urgency with which they wanted to leave.

Gunfire echoed out in the distance as a reminder of the urgency of their departure.

"Let's move, now!" Craven helped Amyn to his feet, and they hobbled out together. The wounded Mamluk shrugged off his assistance as he hauled himself up into the saddle before Craven passed him his sword.

"Why? Why do this for me?"

"After all that you saw and went through at the citadel, you could have gone anywhere, but you came to us, do you know what that tells me?"

Amyn shook his head.

"That you had nowhere else left to go. I know that feeling all too well." Craven leapt onto one of the other horses to see a pistol slung in a holster on the saddle.

"Where did you find these horses?" he asked Hawkshaw.

"From men who will no longer have need of them," declared Birback.

That was all he needed to hear as he addressed Amyn once more.

"You know this place, and you know where we are going. Show us the way, the fastest and quickest way possible."

He looked weak as he held up one hand and could barely support the weight of it. He then pointed up one of the streets. Craven looked around once more only to find several locals looking back with suspicious eyes, as the world felt as though it was collapsing in on them. He had never been so eager to leave a place before.

"Moxy, Caffy, lead the way!"

They launched into a gallop as they sought to escape the city and be on their way, before they were caught by the mob that had swept through the city and seemingly the entire country. It was not long before they left Cairo behind. Paget looked back at the adjacent city of Giza and the pyramids he'd yearned to see but did not complain. For he knew how deadly their situation was and wanted nothing more now than to go North with all haste.

The road to Alexandria was as calm as a busy trade route could be. Carts creaked along the congested route, but at least they were away from the roar of muskets and the cries of bloody murder. They let their horses plod on at a steady pace, which would not exhaust them. Yet they were all aware of the suspicions glances they received. They stood out amongst even all the other foreigners on the route as none wore European dress.

Craven gripped the throat of his scabbard tightly with his left hand, his right with the reins rested near to it, ready to draw the weapon in haste if need be. He looked on at every passer-by with great suspicion, expecting them to attack at any moment.

The day came to a close without incident. They rode on in the darkness for a little while before accepting their horses needed rest. Moxy struck up a fire as quickly as he could, but the night was still warmer than most winter days they had lived through in Portugal recently, and so it was not much of a hardship. A small bag of bread was passed about, the only food they had to sustain themselves. Although somehow Birback had a dozen flasks of wine, which he now shared about. They were much appreciated by all, except Amyn.

"After all you have seen you will still not take a drink?" Craven passed a flask on without taking a sip.

Amyn shook his head and would not hear of it.

"Even if it might ease the weight on your shoulders?"

"I do not believe there is enough wine in all the world to drown out the memories I have of this day. And I would not have them dulled, for this day should not be forgotten."

"There is no coming back for you is there, ever?" Paget asked him.

Amyn said nothing, but they all knew it was true.

"That was the most barbaric display I can imagine. Only in the pages of history can I think of such a thing," declared Hawkshaw.

"Though I have not seen it, news of the massacres in Spain have reached us," Paget added.

"But not the systematic destruction of an entire people."

"Like Rome did to Carthage," Paget replied pensively as he thought back to the stories he had read of the similarly devastating and destructive display that had occurred on the same continent almost two thousand years ago.

"And if I go with you to Portugal, and the English lose, what then?"

"I don't know, but at least you would have a chance of making your own destiny. For there is only certain death if you stayed here," replied Craven.

"In England there are great contests of swordsmen like you, where men are bruised and bloodied for sport and for money," added Matthys as he tried to find some way to support. The foreigner would stand in stark contrast to all the Europeans they would mingle with.

Amyn sighed.

"You would have me fight for others' entertainment when my people used to rule all these lands?"

"A king is not a king anymore when he loses his kingdom," declared Paget.

Exhaustion soon set in, for they had all endured the most gruelling of days. Not just on their bodies, but on their minds. They soon settled in for the night, huddled under the stars amongst the few coats and blankets they had between them. The bustle of the travellers along the road woke them as the first rays of light shone on the horizon. They gathered their few things as they continued on. Amyn already appeared stronger, and yet he still limped and sighed with pain as he got into the saddle.

"How far will they pursue you?" Craven asked as they went on, having so little to collect up that they went from sleep to saddle in just a few minutes.

"To the furthest of Pasha's reach, the borders of this country, and perhaps a little beyond. They have tried to end my people since all my years and many before me. And now they have succeeded. They will be sure there is never a return."

"Then do not fight to return. Do not chase what you can never have."

"But I am still Mamluk," he seethed.

"And you always will be. You do not have to forget where

you came from but look forward. I never imagined myself a soldier, not a real one, and yet it is what I have become."

"And that is what you would have for me?"

"Your people have been soldiers for hundreds of years. You have lost your army and your cause, but I am offering you a new one."

"To fight for a country I do not know?"

"No, for us. Look at these men who now ride with you. You need not fight for England but fight for them. I cannot give you a country, but I can give you a brotherhood."

Amyn smiled even through his pain and the loss, which weighed so heavily on him, but he did not reply. Craven came to a halt as he heard the sound of galloping horses approaching with such urgency, it warranted attention. He pulled the blanket which rested over his head to cover his Western attire and watched with suspicion as two riders rushed along the line of travellers. He looked away a little as they approached, but they soon slowed. They seemed to recognise something was off about Craven and his party. They came to a standstill and approached slowly as one of them yelled at the group.

Craven knew their cover was blown as he looked to Amyn who seemed to fear he would be given up. But Craven only smiled back. He did not hesitate to draw out the pistol from his saddle and shoot the first one, as Moxy's rifle rang out a second after, and the other was blown from his saddle. Amyn drew out his sword as the one Craven had shot still reached for his own sword, despite the hole in his chest. Amyn hacked him down with a single and swift killing blow before looking back at Craven in surprise.

"I didn't know you were true until now," he declared.

"We are in this together now, and we will be so long as you desire it."

Craven looked about them all. Those on the road continued to walk past the bodies without any care for them, not wanting to get involved. Many dared not touch them whilst others soon began to take anything of value.

"How could you know they were a threat to us?" Hawkshaw finally found his words, having been stunned by the sudden display of violence.

"Anyone on the lookout for Europeans now means to do us harm."

"You don't know that."

"Come on, you saw the same as the rest of us what happened back in Cairo. If someone presents any danger to you between here and the sea, you better be damned certain you put them down before they don't give you a chance," snapped Craven as he led them on.

It was a bitter thing to swallow, and yet deep down Hawkshaw knew he was right.

"Trust in Craven. He has gotten us this far, which few men would have," insisted Paget as they rode side by side.

"After all I had read of Craven and his adventures, I had thought them to be great heroic endeavours, not this."

"But they are, and yet there are times in between which no one would want to write about in the newspapers."

They rode on for the rest of the day without incident before making camp once more; knowing the next day would see their escape to safety if they could just make it to the coast.

"Do you trust Captain Payne to have waited for us?" Paget spoke quietly to Craven.

"I trust him to wait long enough to get paid, yes."

Amyn fell silent that evening, the sorrow and horrors he had witnessed weighing heavily on him. The rest of them had witnessed it, but they did not know those who fell like family. Craven imagined what it must be like. He placed himself in Amyn's shoes, imagining what he would think if he had seen all the friends around him die before his eyes. It was hard to envisage such a possibility, and yet even trying to do so caused a great rage to build up inside of him. He knew he must stop and tried to think of better days, only to find his mind leading him to thoughts of Major Bouchard.

"Now will you kill him?" Birback demanded who seemingly saw right through Craven and into his thoughts.

"Who?" Paget had not cottoned on what he meant.

"Major Bouchard, we all saw him," replied Matthys.

"I'll kill him all right, when the time is right," growled Craven.

"And when is that?" Paget asked.

"The time was right the moment you had him by the balls," replied Birback scathingly, causing Amyn to chime into the conversation with much curiosity.

"You had a chance to kill a man who had wronged you greatly, and you hesitated?"

"I did not hesitate!"

"Then why did you not kill him?"

"Because he was sickly, and it wasn't a fair fight," replied Paget in respect of Craven's decision.

"Fair? If I had a chance to stab Muhammad Pasha in the back or slit his throat, I would not hesitate."

"But I am not you, and this is my battle to face. I will deal with the Major on my own terms, Amyn."

"All the while he is free to go about his business and cause havoc for the rest of us," complained Birback.

"Another would only replace him. All things in good time," replied Matthys.

"One more day, and we will be away from this place," muttered Paget wearily.

"You couldn't get here more quickly," smiled Charlie.

"And perhaps I shall return one day under better circumstances. I would come here as a tourist, not whatever this is, not as a hunted man."

It was easy to fall asleep once more after a full day's ride, but not for Amyn. He could not hold his eyes shut as thoughts and memories flooded his mind for several hours. He was restless and needed to relieve himself. The fire still crackled and shone in between them, and so he got up and moved further into the darkness when he heard footsteps. He went silent as he stopped, looking down for his sword. He had left it at the fire side, having only a small knife on his belt, which he reached for but did not draw. He heard another footstep as a boot pressed down ever so gently on soft foliage, but it was enough to cause him to turn and draw out his knife. He saw the dark shadows of three men before him. The faintest moonlight glistened off the blades they carried, the same kind of short curved kilij sword he favoured and used all through the Ottoman Empire and amongst the Mamluks. They approached as assassins in the night, and he was in no doubt of this mission as they slowly approached him, one of them grinning maniacally as if to savour the kill.

The assassins stopped as Amyn spread both his hands,

one with the short blade, and the other empty, as he tried to ward himself against all three, despite the odds being stacked heavily against him, especially in his weakened state. Amyn muttered a prayer to himself as he called on the strength of his god to see him through. Yet after the slaughter of his people, he wondered if it was worth anything at all and so stopped, as he slowed his breathing and focused his mind. He knew the chance of survival was incredibly slim, and yet he was ready to make their lives hell in his last moments.

He was ready to die, yet a fourth figure suddenly emerged from the darkness behind the three assassins and drove a sword into the back of one, deep into his body so he was killed instantly. The dead body dropped, leaving his killer in his place. It was Caffy who looked upon Amyn with a smile, knowing he had given him a fighting chance, as he picked up the dead man's sword and tossed it to Amyn.

The sadistic looking one who had grinned at Amyn so gleefully now turned his attention to Caffy. He rushed at the newcomer, but the muscular and burly former slave lifted up his French sabre and brought it down with such tremendous force it passed through the assassin's sword. The blade snapped near the hilt, as Caffy's blade struck his head like a butcher's cleaver. It chopped through his turban and down to his eyebrows in a devastating display of his strength, causing both Amyn and the last assassin to pause in awe of the display.

The last man looked from Caffy to Amyn who now had a sword in one hand and dagger in the other. He waited only a brief second before turning his back and running as quickly as he could. Yet Amyn tossed his dagger after the man, embedding it in his back between his shoulder blades, and causing him to crash to the ground. Amyn was on him in a flash, pulling his head up from the ground and slitting his throat with his sword. He then threw it down beside the body and retrieved his dagger. He remembered the man who had saved him and got up to face off against him, almost wondering if he had an ulterior motive.

"Why? Why risk yourself for me?"

He seemed as calm as could be, as he wiped the blood off his sword in the dead man's clothing, before sheathing his weapon and squaring off against Amyn.

"Why?" replied Caffy in astonishment and surprise.

"You do not owe me anything."

"You are one of us now."

Amyn sighed in frustration.

"Do you know how many of your kind I have traded?" he replied, as if feeling guilty for having received help from a former slave.

"We have all done many things. I only care what you do now," replied Caffy as he hinted at his own experiences and things he would not so readily admit.

"Tell me, are you really one of them, one of Craven's blades? The Salford Rifles?" Amyn probed, as Caffy looked nothing like the rest of them and was as much an outsider as he was.

"Captain Craven cares only about two things. That you can fight, and you can be trusted."

"What the hell is this?" Craven's voice called out as he and Paget approached, drawing their swords.

"We had some visitors," smiled Amyn.

"Nothing we could not handle," added Caffy as he nodded towards Amyn.

"Is everyone in this damned country trying to kill us?" Paget muttered.

"Are we all good?" Craven asked.

"There was one more who held the horses of these men," replied Caffy.

"Where?"

"He was the first to die," declared Caffy, causing Amyn's eyebrow to raise, as he realised Caffy's efforts were even more than he had seen.

"How many more will come for you?" Craven asked Amyn.

"They will not stop hunting the last of my people until we have left this country."

"And after that?" Paget asked.

"Once all of Egypt is in the clutches of Pasha, I believe he will soon forget us."

"He could not have negotiated for you to leave?"

"And if a usurper asked you to negotiate your banishment from your homeland, would you entertain such a conversation?"

"Never," admitted Paget proudly as he finally understood.

"This country might have been your home once, but not any longer," Craven added quietly.

"Yes, I know that," replied Amyn with great sorrow.

"Gather the horses. We have rested long enough. If those men were able to find us, then so too will many more. I would be out to sea before noon tomorrow," declared Craven.

CHAPTER 15

Hawkshaw yawned and rubbed his weary eyes. The sun was now high in the sky, and they had been on the road for many hours, with only the most modest amount of sleep. It was clear he was not yet accustomed to the rough life of a soldier on campaign, and yet Benning seemed most at home as if he had lived this way his entire life.

"There it is."

Craven came to a halt as they gazed upon Alexandria, which now seemed a far more magnificent sight than the Pyramids themselves. They could see the ocean and the masts of vessels and hoped they may escape with their lives. They rode on, relieved that they were on the home stretch. The near two weeks at sea seemed a welcome rest to Craven now, as he welcomed a night's rest when he did not have to keep one eye open, and fear being stabbed in the back. Yet as they closed in towards the city limits, they could see a body of twenty or more cavalrymen excitedly pointing and shouting towards them.

"Don't do it, we are this close," muttered Moxy.

But they had no such luck, as several of the cavalrymen drew swords and rushed on at them.

"Move!" Craven kept his horse directed towards the city and galloped forward. He hoped to get to the shelter of the city before their pursuers attempted to cut them off.

Moxy lifted his long rifle and quickly shot one from the saddle before riding on after the rest of them.

"All this for one man?" Paget was amazed that such an effort would be made to pursue Amyn.

"It is the difference between the Governor laying the claim of killing all the Mamluks in Cairo and not!" Amyn yelled.

"You're too stubborn to die," smiled Craven as they raced onward as fast as their horses would carry them.

Gunfire rang out as the cavalrymen fired upon them, but to no effect. They could hardly aim as they galloped along in pursuit, yet Moxy still ducked down low and cursed as he heard a ball whiz past his head.

"How can they be travelling faster from Cairo than us?"

"Those men are not from Cairo!" Amyn shouted back to Paget.

It was a terrifying thought to know they were not just being pursued, but that they were now wanted men across the entire country. They soon reached the first streets of the city and galloped down a long winding road. Craven finally brought them to a standstill and directed his horse into a small side street. The others followed suit, some with him and the rest in an opposing alley.

"We have to stand and fight," insisted Hawkshaw.

"Fight, yes, but on our terms. Moxy, you're the fox," he ordered, knowing the hunter would know precisely what he was asking for.

The Welshman rode out from cover and ambled a few paces further along the street. He looked back for the enemy and waited for them to catch a glimpse of him. It only took a few seconds before he dug in his heels and continued on along the street. Paget waited anxiously for the enemy to approach, expecting to be seen by them, for they were only a few paces from the road. He looked to Craven to show his concern, but Craven shook his head to demand he not move.

They could feel the thunderous charge of the cavalry through the saddles of their own horses. They finally they came into view and galloped on without a glance either side to where Paget and the others took refuge. The Turkish troops stormed on in column, disorganised and out of formation, as a result of the narrow streets and the hectic pursuit.

"Give people a big enough target to focus their attention, and they are blind to all else." Craven smiled as he guided his horse back onto the road.

He rushed on after the cavalry who gave pursuit to Moxy. Craven drew out his blade as the others rushed on in pursuit. Amyn seemed especially in good spirits as he shrugged off the pain and weakness in his body. He eagerly pursued what little revenge he might get as they turned the tables on their pursuers.

Craven was soon upon the tail man at the end of the cavalry. He went unnoticed as he approached and thrust his blade through his body, quickly retracting it as the man slumped over the saddle and fell from it. He went on and hacked down on the back of the next one, felling him just as quickly. Amyn overtook him and slashed a long drawn out cut down the back of the next man before going on as they worked to even the odds.

The next man in the cavalry column look back just in time to see Amyn's blade slash across his face, but the blow caused him to be launched sideways off the saddle, and he crashed into a stack of ceramic jugs. It brought the attention of the next man along. Amyn hacked down and rushed forward before he could cry out. He hacked down against his sword arm, finishing him with another blow to the face. But another two ahead had noticed the ruckus and looked back. They saw Amyn and Craven and the others in full view. The game was up, but a tight bend in the road forced them all to hang on tightly to their saddles, as they came about and quickly drew to a halt.

They had found the road blocked by a cart. Moxy had left his horse and was fighting up a narrow stairway, using his long rifle like a big club as he kept three men at bay. They had tried to rush up and reach him, only to have their numbers stifled by the narrow entrance.

Horses reared up as several turned about and their riders cried out to alert the others to those approaching. But Amyn did not give them time to collect themselves and reform. He set upon the first and hacked down across his body with a ferocious blow.

Craven took the reins in his sword hand as he pulled the pistol out from his saddle. He shot another at near point-blank range before throwing the pistol at another. He took hold of the reins with his bridle hand once more and attacked the one he had thrown it at. He cut down with several blows but found his blade beaten aside. He then followed with a thrust, which caught the soldier completely by surprise as it sailed through his seemingly strong guard and embedded in his chest. Yet before he could draw it away, another of the soldiers slashed against his arm. It was not a blow with huge force, but the long drawing motion cut right through his coat sleeve and sliced deeply into his sword arm.

Craven grimaced from the pain but fought his best to ignore it. He speedily yanked his own sword from the man he had stabbed and cut into the next attack levelled at his face. Paget ran him through as he saw his Captain struggling.

The rest of Craven's small unit ran amok against the Turkish troops in a roughly even contest in numbers, although the Turkish troops were no match for the highly skilled swordfighters surrounding Craven. He watched as they went to work, hacking and slashing their way through those who had pursued them, until the last remaining few pushed their way out of the fight to try and escape.

Benning caught one across the throat with such a blow so as to take the man's head clean off. His horse then rode on with his body still in the saddle. Two of them escaped, leaving only two remaining on the stairs where they struggled to reach Moxy. They were unfortunate to be oblivious to the devastation of their comrades as riderless horses ambled about amongst the dead littering the ground.

Amyn approached the stairs with a murderous swagger, his sword held low with no care or concern for his enemy at all. One turned to face him as he approached, but he merely ducked down low and slashed up, cleaving the man across the body. The other turned in horror to realise he was the last standing, and the bloodthirsty Amyn glaring back at him. But it was the butt of

Moxy's rifle that smashed the last soldier in the head and caused him to crumple to the ground. The Welshman slowly breathed a sigh of relief that it was all over, as he descended the stairs and leapt over the body triumphantly.

"Is there something wrong with your sword?" Birback asked him.

"When you've got three savages after your skin, you would want to keep them at length, too," he answered with a beaming smile.

But Matthys turned his attention to Craven who was checking his wound and found blood gushing from it. He was struggling to sheath his sabre as his strength began to fail.

"We've been here quite long enough," roared Craven as he turned his focus to their urgent escape.

"Those men who escaped will surely soon return with more," added Paget.

"Then let us be on our way!"

Caffy and Birback shoved the cart out of the road as Amyn and Moxy quickly leapt onto their horses without even time for Moxy to reload his rifle, but more eager to flee than worry about it.

"Lead the way," Craven ordered to Amyn.

None of the others had any clue where they were in the tight confines of the streets of Alexandria. They had no points of reference with which to judge how they might reach the sea. Amyn led them forward at a trot. It was the most their horses could manage now. Many people leapt aside and yelled abuse at them as they forced their way through the busy streets. Some even seemed to call out Amyn, as if knowing he was an open target for all. But nobody dared make any attempt to do him harm, as the bloodied and ruthless looking escort remained close to him. Craven rode with his sword in his left hand; ready to strike at anyone who dared try and cause them any difficulty or violent intent.

The journey seemed to go on forever as they passed through a maze of winding streets of the bustling city. They carefully watched every side road and alley with much suspicion, as if expecting to be attacked. It caused so much stress on their already exhausted minds and bodies until the streets opened up before them, and they had their first glimpse of the water. At last, they could taste the salt of the ocean, which was the taste of freedom they had dreaded they would never reach.

They rode along the waterfront. Craven suddenly came to a halt as he noticed Captain Payne sitting under an umbrella with his feet up on a barrel and a glass of wine in his hand. He looked most rested and living the high life, as he was waited upon with several of his crew. They all appeared to be as calm as could be. Payne put his glass down as he slapped his thigh and began to clap. A huge smile stretched across his face.

"Captain Craven, your return brings me great joy. For now, I get paid a second time!" He picked up his wine and held it up to toast his financial success.

"I would have us underway immediately if you are to be certain of ever receiving that payment," declared Craven.

"Oh, come now, Captain, what can possibly be the rush?"

He slowly took a bottle from the table and began to fill his glass once more. But the sound of galloping horses and a ruckus in the street along the way caused many to turn to see what the commotion was all about. A rider with his sword drawn pointed his weapon towards Amyn and the rest of them, as he ordered his troop on. Payne downed his glass before smashing it on the ground.

"Time to be on our way," he insisted with urgency. He rushed out towards the boats hauled ashore on the bay nearby, but carefully keeping his bottle in hand. Craven and the rest of them rushed their horses to the boats as if to leave without him. Meanwhile, the old American ran on to catch up with the few crew he had.

"Damn it!" he roared as the cavalry galloped by. He looked at his wine bottle, sad to see it go, and tossed it at one of the passing troopers. The bottle smashed cross his face and knocked him from his horse. He landed unconscious before Payne drew out his old hanger from his soldiering days and rushed towards the commotion, as Craven's comrades pushed a boat out into the water.

Birback and Benning waited with swords in hand to oppose the cavalry who dismounted to follow them into the water. Steel clashed as the first of them reached Benning. He quickly snapped a cut at the soldier's hand left exposed by the lack of ward iron. The lash opened a deep cut across several fingers and the back of the hand, causing him to drop the sword as he withdrew to safety. Birback looked impressed, but now took his turn to one-up the officer. He swung towards the head of one of the enemies, causing him to draw up his sword for defence. He was unable to move his feet so quickly in the water, and Birback lashed a cut down at his leg. He crashed down into the water as blood poured out from the wound.

Yet the rest of the troops rushed on them, and Birback was cut across his left arm as he struck from one side to the other.

"That's not even my boat!" Payne yelled, as he stormed out into the water before realising he didn't need to play any part in it. He went for his own, and he and his crew pushed out into the water, not getting any attention from the soldiers. They were not their intended target.

"Come on!" Craven clambered aboard, his arm barely having enough strength to support his weight as he stood up in the boat. Hawkshaw rushed back to help his man, as Caffy and Charlie took out oars, using them to beat the soldiers back as they withdrew further into the water. Paget tumbled into the boat after Craven, whilst Matthys and Joze kept pushing them further out into deeper water.

"Let's go. Now, move it!" Craven ordered.

Charlie handed the oar to Paget who was on the bow, which he used to furiously swing back and forth as the others climbed in. He got one clean hit with a horizontal swing. It smashed one soldier in the face, and he collapsed down into the water, just as another came forward. Paget drew out his sword and beat down against the man with multiple furious blows, before remembering it would do no good as it had no edge, but it was enough to keep him at bay. As they began to row into deeper depths, the soldiers could no longer stand in the deep water, and they were forced to withdraw in frustration. Paget slumped down into the boat with a sigh of relief. As they began to catch up with Payne, they could see he and his crew casually went on with no worries in the world.

"They are going for a boat!" Joze pointed back to the coastline to see the soldiers take to the water after them. There were more than a dozen of them, with more arriving at the water's edge to commandeer another boat.

"Faster!" Payne cried out, suddenly realising the danger they were all in.

They all put their backs into it as both boats rushed to reach the Margaretta. Payne got to his feet and shouted out towards the vessel, waving his hands frantically.

"Weigh anchor! Weigh anchor!"

Paget watched anxiously from the prow of the boat at the enemy approaching, knowing it would take some time to get their ship underway, as Moxy finished loading his rifle and took aim. The mass of troops in the boat seemed impossible to miss, but as he pulled the trigger, the boat rocked over a modest wave and his shot flew over their heads.

"You picked a hell of a time to miss," quipped Craven.

Moxy was seething as he began to reload once more, intent on hitting his target. They were drawing up near to the vessel when he finished loading and rested the muzzle on the edge of the boat. This time he took careful aim.

"Wait!"

He demanded they all remain still for him to take the shot. He held his breath and took the shot. Once again, the gentle rock of the boat played havoc with his aim. The ball skimmed the arm of one of those rowing, who shrugged it off as if it was a horsefly.

"Waste of bloody time," complained Craven as he began to climb up the side of the Margaretta. Although he could only hang his right arm through the ropes as he used his left and his feet to keep moving upward.

They left the boat floating beside them as Captain Payne came alongside the ship. The crew began to lash the boat to haul it aboard as the sails were released, and they hurried to get underway. Moxy was aboard for only a single second when he took his rifle from his back and proceeded to load a third shot. His intent was to at least land one as the others looked out at the enemy closing in on them.

"They will reach us before we can get away," said Paget.

"What are they going to do now?" Hawkshaw asked from their high position, as if in a castle tower looking down on the poor fellows assaulting it. But Craven pointed to two more boats heading out towards them.

"They only need slow us down long enough, and we will be in real trouble." He looked around at his bloodied and exhausted friends, his own arm trailing by his side, now useless.

"We have to slow them down, Sir."

"And we will," replied Payne as he disappeared into his Captain's cabin. He returned a few moments later brandishing a marvellous musket with the most ludicrous of short bronze mortar barrels that could fire a charge the size of a fist. It looked like a comedic device for the theatre, as if a tiny cannon barrel had been mounted into the butt and lock of a Land Pattern musket. He cocked the lock and held it up on target, elevating the barrel somewhat to aim slightly above his target.

The others watched on in surprise as he pulled the trigger. The powder flashed, and an immense burst of flame and smoke engulfed the American as the large charge burst out. It was at such a low velocity they could see the huge ball soar towards the boat in a great arc. It began to dip, and several of the Turkish troops leapt overboard in horror of the sight just as it crashed into the boat, landing amongst them. All aboard the Margaretta watched in amazement as if expecting a great explosion. They looked to Payne for an answer as he just rested the mini mortar across his arms and waited patiently.

"Is that it?" Birback asked.

But the Turks began yelling out in a panic. They reversed their oars and began to paddle back towards the coastline. Others began to bilge water out with their bare hands, as the boat took on water at a great speed. They began to lower in the water quickly, as Benning led the cheer at their success, and applause rang out from the deck of the Margaretta. The sails began to take wind, and they set on their way as the other boats went to the rescue of the sinking one, and the men were forced to take to the water.

"I would not visit this port again anytime soon," declared Craven to the American.

"I just saved your lives, and you don't forget it."

"You saved yourself and your payday!"

"Can a man not have many motivations?" Payne smiled back at Craven.

Matthys was soon beside Craven, checking him over as blood continued to pour from the wound. The Sergeant looked down to see it pooling on the deck below the Captain, and he looked back up. Craven was pale and gaunt looking, and he suddenly dropped. Matthys succeeded in catching him just before his head would have bounced from the deck.

CHAPTER 16

Craven opened his eyes in what felt like the first time in a long time, and yet he'd had feverish dreams. He suddenly felt a little sick, but when he looked around, he realised he was hanging in a hammock. He groaned at the realisation they were still at sea. He was soaked through with sweat and eager to get out of it, as he leaned out and then fell out tumbling to the ground. His limbs were stiff, but he was relieved to find his right arm had as much strength as the rest of his limbs when he struggled back to his feet. He grabbed the sheet and wiped himself clean before pulling on the clothes that were hung nearby. His coat still bore the deep cut which had lost him so much blood. He could see his sword belt and dagger hanging nearby but decided to leave them where they were. He then went up on deck, to the shock and astonishment of a troubled looking Paget. He sprung to life upon first sight of him and embraced him like a long-lost father.

"It is surely so good to see you up and about, Sir!"

Most of his comrades were on deck and looked equally as surprised to see him, if not quite so enthusiastic as the Lieutenant.

"How long have I been out?"

"Nine days, Sir," replied Paget as if he had been carefully counting.

"Good. Then I missed most of the voyage," declared Craven who was already sick of being at sea, despite having witnessed only a few minutes of their time on the water.

"How do you feel?" Matthys asked.

"Like I died."

"That cut was the least of your troubles. It was the fever that took you. How could you have gone on like that without letting me see to your wound?"

"There was no time. The only thing that mattered was getting out of that damned country." He then noticed Amyn was with them and suddenly looked a little sheepish.

"No offence intended," he added.

"You are not wrong, my friend, for I should never want to see it again either. It is awash with the blood of my people and the soldiers of my enemy."

"I've never known such an effort launched to take down one man."

"Well, we know that's not true, Sir."

Craven waited for an explanation from Paget.

"Major Bouchard and his mission? You were their target. The resources it must have taken to go after you, Sir. You cannot forget that."

"My survival makes a mockery of the Governor," added Amyn.

"Then we should make sure people far and wide know it."

Amyn shook his head at Craven.

"I would have it remain in the past. Sore memories are best left behind, and I would not have all of you pursued in my name."

"Nobody will pursue you in Portugal nor Spain," declared Craven.

"What now, Sir?" Paget asked excitedly.

"Our mission was a success, remarkably. Let us return to the army and do what we should be doing."

"Driving the French from Portugal?"

"Yes, and through Spain and all the way back to Paris!"

Hawkshaw cheered in support as the ship's Captain joined them.

"Thank you, together we made it through," announced Craven.

"I didn't sit around waiting for nothing, to lose my ship and my bounty. I will see you safely back to Lisbon, and I will be paid handsomely for it."

Craven smiled and nodded in appreciation at both the honesty and the hustle.

"So what now, Sir?" Paget asked again.

"How long until we reach Lisbon?"

"Three days," replied Payne.

"Then bring us some single sticks, for I need to regain my strength."

"Do you have any?" Paget asked the Captain.

"As it happens, I do." He nodded towards one of his crewmen to retrieve them, "It might surprise you that it so happens I was once quite the swordsman myself."

Craven smiled as the crewman returned with a pair of the wooden training tools, which looked well battered from regular usage.

"Let us see it, then," smiled Craven as he took them and threw one at the Captain, forcing him to catch it.

"You are in no condition for such exertion."

"Indeed, and so you might have a chance."

Somehow, he managed to tap into a competitive streak seemingly buried deep down in the American's soul, as he was angered by the sentiment and held up the stick in guard, ready to take on the challenge.

"Take it easy," insisted Matthys.

"When have you ever known me to do that?" Craven smiled at him.

Payne felt the pressure being put upon him as his crew looked on excitedly to see the contest. And so he gave in to the pressure and took up the singlestick. Matthys watched with concern for the Captain's wounds and general health.

"Are you going to let this happen?" Hawkshaw asked him; now understanding the Sergeant was Craven's voice of reason and counsel.

"I am afraid there are limits to my ability to make the Captain do anything."

Craven smiled as he circled the American. He could feel his legs getting stronger with every step, as they worked off the sleepiness of more than a week's inactivity. He still felt some pain in his arm, but his strength was returning, as he clenched tightly about the stick to test the strength he would need to parry and strike.

Finally, he flourished a figure of eight with the stick, in

what seemed like showing off and taunting his opponent. In reality, it was only one more way he tested his own strength and loosened his stiff body. The American waited for him to make the first move, and Craven began to wonder why.

"Don't go easy on me."

"Don't you worry about that. I won't."

Craven decided to test the waters first. He swung the stick into a rotation to make a feint before rotating through into a strike. He was surprised to find that Payne snapped a cut in during his rotations in a perfect timed action, which would incapacitate many a fighter immediately. Craven spotted it just in time and whirled his stick about, taking the blow on the leather basket. He smiled at the attempt to shrug it off, and yet the truth was he wondered if he would have stopped the blow, had it not been for the protective bowl about his hand. Craven began to wonder if the American just had a natural response like a cudgeller, or if he truly was a well skilled swordsman. He feinted down towards his leg and got no response at all, and that told him everything he needed to know. For a swordsman with quick reactions who doesn't respond to a feint is both skilled and confident.

Next Craven threw multiple feints with the smallest of movements so as not to leave any openings with which Payne could respond. He finally launched his cut to the face, only to find it parried with ease. A cut was snapped back towards him, and he was forced to withdraw and take it on the stick.

"You've had some training," announced Craven.

"I didn't get this far in life with only my words."

Craven appreciated the sentiment as he attacked again. Payne took a parry before pushing a thrust through his guard, but it went far wide of the left side of his face. And yet the miss was intentional to draw away his guard, as the American snapped the stick back. It struck Craven on the cheek with what would be the back edge of the blade. It was a light strike that caused only a small mark, although they both knew it would have opened up a nasty gash had the same been done with a double-edged blade. But he took it in his stride as he went back on the attack. A masterful display was put on for the audience who watched with glee, as strike after strike was made and returned. Not a hit landed for a full minute until both men withdrew to take a breather.

"How is he doing it?" Paget was shocked that the American was able to match Craven, who was still recovering from his wounds and ailments, and yet appeared remarkably strong in the contest.

"There were fine swordsmen in England long before your Captain." Payne smiled, having heard Paget allude to the experience he had.

"Why does a great swordsman no longer live by the blade?" Craven asked.

"We all get old, and there are more ways to make money than with the blade."

"And is that the only reason to use a blade?"

"No, for they are awfully fun." Payne smiled again as he went back on the attack with the vitality of a much younger man. Craven's strength began to fail him from over exertion in his recovering state. The American struck him a smarting blow across his right knee, which lowered his guard. He wrapped another one over his head only for Craven to growl angrily in response. He rushed forward; beat Payne's stick aside, kicked his front foot out from him, and shoved him over. He crashed hard onto the deck, the wind being taken out of him as his stick flew from his hands, and Craven presented his own singlestick to the Captain's chest.

Payne groaned for a moment before seeing Craven's stern expression as though he wanted blood, before both men began to laugh. Craven knelt down and offered a hand to help him to his feet, even though he wobbled and shook a little as he hauled Payne upright. Paget began to clap in appreciation for the display. The others joined in, and they passed the sticks over to one of the crew as the audience faded away.

"You've got quite some fight still left in you," declared Craven to the older man who had fought in wars before Craven was even born.

"Those are not the bones of a man who no longer practices," declared Matthys as he gently enquired as to the Captain's abilities.

"A good fighter never stops training," he admitted.

"Then this character you play, it is an act?" Paget asked at the American's seemingly drunken and slovenly lifestyle.

"A half-truth," smiled Payne. He looked back to see Craven slump down and rest his aching body, as he felt for small cut on his head and found fresh blood.

"It is lucky you have a few days' rest left before you return to service. For if it had been a Frenchman with a sabre who had done that, you would no longer be for this world."

"There are very few Frenchmen I have ever encountered who could make such a fight as that."

"I used to be like you, Craven, and I sought out the finest swordsmen to learn from and test my skills. I contested with every strong Highlander I could find and many sergeants of the finest dragoon regiments. Fencing masters and stage gladiators, and anyone who may present a challenge."

Craven listened in with much curiosity now, and yet he was not surprised to hear it, not after the display of skill he had witnessed and the hardships he had faced.

"And now?"

"I will always have time for the sword and the art which adorns it. For nothing in fencing is certain; but the art one employs renders it both useful and agreeable."

Craven was astonished as he had heard such words before but never would have expected them from an old American rogue out on the sea looking to make his fortune.

"So why did you leave the service?"

"Because war is a young man's game, or at least the fighting of it with one's own hands are. I had my war and we lost, but life goes on. I have found my life out here, just as you have found yours."

"What do you mean?"

"I know you, Craven, probably better than you know yourself, because I was you. You found something in Portugal, which you didn't know you needed, and now you move with a singular purpose. Hold on to that, for it is a rare thing to find."

Craven nodded in agreement as he looked around at the friends who were by his side through hell and back.

"Now, rest up, for I imagine when we reach Lisbon you will have some hard days of riding and fighting ahead."

* * *

Craven watched with anticipation and joy as they came into Lisbon harbour. He stretched out his body and rolled his shoulder. He clenched his fists as he felt his strength returned and dry land was once more in sight, for he would take a week on the road in Portugal over another night at sea. The port was filled with merchant vessels coming and going, and yet comparatively few British troops were visible from the port.

"Has the army finally marched North, Sir?" Paget asked excitedly.

"They had to. For any more inactivity, and Wellington would have been recalled to London. And we all would have been sent home."

Soon enough they were at the harbour side and descending the plank onto firm ground, with Captain Payne and a large party of his crew following them ashore.

"I imagine you come for supplies?" Craven asked him.

"I came to get the monies which are owed to me."

"Then it was good to see you again, Captain. An unexpected experience, but a most welcome one."

"Good luck to you, then," he replied before parting ways.

They returned to the warehouse where they had traded their uniforms for what they now wore. They found it was under guard by two Portuguese militiamen who recognised Craven instantly and opened the doors for them. Stepping inside they found the room just as they had left it, and it was sighs of relief echoing out as they stripped off their equipment and took back what was their own. Craven looked down at his sword with the relief of seeing a great friend after many years apart. As he put on his sword belt about his waist and pulled on his tunic, he noticed Amyn standing idly by, being the only one who had not set out from Lisbon with them.

Craven went along a clothes rack until he found a redcoat in respectable condition. He took it to him and pushed it into Amyn's hands, forcing him to take it. He at first looked insulted by having the garment thrust into him, but then looked down at the scarlet jacket and realised what it meant.

"You would have me wear this?" he asked in disbelief.

"I would be honoured if you would. I cannot imagine what it must feel like to lose all that you have, but I am offering you a new path. The men who follow me are two things above all else. They are loyal, and they are great fighters. I cannot imagine a better place for you to be."

"You have the power to do this?

"If he were any other captain, no, but this is Craven, and this is the Salford Rifles. He can do whatever he wants," added Paget.

Amyn took off the blanket he has used to keep himself warm. He then ripped the rags that were the tunic he had worn upon his escape from Cairo and slipped into the tunic. He still wore the huge bellowing green pantaloons, and his turban and was unmistakable amongst the others. Yet as he buttoned up the tunic, he sighed in relief and contentment realising he had found a new home.

"I can't promise you riches or an easy life, but I can give you this. Join us, as a brother." Craven picked up a rifle and handed it to Amyn.

"Do you know how to use that?" Moxy joked.

"I have hunted beasts that would tear you limb from limb," he replied as he took the weapon and a cartridge box from a nearby table. Craven handed him a greatcoat, too.

"If the army marches North, I would have us arrive before they meet the French in open battle," insisted Craven.

"Is that what you seek now?" Hawkshaw asked.

"I promised our Portuguese friends that I would see the French out of their country, and I mean to keep my word. And we have friends who march towards that end even now, so let us not leave them to do it alone." He grabbed the last of his equipment and headed out of the door to go for the stables to retrieve their horses, where they found Captain Payne approaching with some urgency.

"What is it?" Craven asked.

"Word has just come in of Badajoz. It has fallen."

"Badajoz?" Paget gasped as he thought of the Spanish fortress that they had all hoped would hold out for many more months.

"Then the East is fallen, and our flank is weak. We must reach the army with all urgency and ensure a fatal blow is delivered to Masséna, before he can rally, and we face two French armies. Thank you, Captain."

"Good luck, Craven."

They again parted ways, and they rushed to the stables. Paget led the way with such eagerness as to be reunited with his beloved Augustus. He soon found his friend and greeted him with a warm welcome.

"Get that saddle on!"

Craven moved with urgency, quickly negotiating a few coins with one of the stable hands to secure a mount for Amyn. In just a few short moments they were ready to ride and were rushing out onto the road. Paget continued to console his friend for the weeks they had been apart.

"How do we know where to go, Sir?" Paget asked.

"We follow that." He pointed to a line of carts transporting supplies North. They rode on but had only been on the road for a matter of minutes when they spotted Major Thornhill. He was approaching from the East. Hawkshaw and a group of his cavalry were following close behind him. They came to a halt beside him.

"What news of Cairo?" he demanded with no pleasantries.

"There will be no aid for this war, not for us nor the French," admitted Craven.

That only seemed to take a small weight off of the Major's mind.

"You should know, Sir, we just received word upon our arrival that Badajoz has fallen."

Thorny grit his teeth and nodded in agreement.

"I will ride North to bring this news to Wellington, would you escort me?" He moved on before hearing an answer, as if expecting them to follow

"And you?" Craven asked Hawkshaw.

"My regiment is required elsewhere, but I must thank you, Captain, for a most insightful few weeks." He smiled before tipping his hat and riding on.

Craven rushed to catch up with Thorny, as they were eager for the Major's insight, which he soon provided as they caught up.

"Your Salford men march with Wellington North, across the hinterland of this country, a most inhospitable place, particularly in this season for which we suffer the last remnants of winter."

"What would you have us do?"

"The only thing we can do. We ride North to see Masséna out of the country."

"There is something else you should know."

"Yes?"

"Major Bouchard, he was there in Cairo."

"And did you kill him?"

"The opportunity did not present itself. We were lucky to get out with our lives."

The Major looked stunned, having no knowledge of the slaughter they had witnessed, but there would be plenty of time on the road to explain it as they hurried to catch the army.

Over many days and much time spent around campfires they shared a great deal of news that had occurred in the month they had been away. After the inactivity over the winter, it seemed as though everything was now moving all at once as they hurried to be part of it.

After six days on the road, they finally reached the rear of the army. They rushed on to Wellington's headquarters without being challenged, with the Major at their head. He and Craven leapt from their horses and passed into Wellington's tent. The General was deliberating with several others about a map. He looked troubled but also welcomed their return.

"Leave us," he insisted. The tent soon emptied, leaving only the three of them. He was eager to hear any fresh news in private, as Major Thornhill slumped down into a chair.

"Badajoz has fallen."

Wellington sighed as he looked back to his map.

"We cannot bother ourselves with that now, but we must frustrate all communication from Alameda and Ciudad

Rodrigo."

"The same old places we fight over again," sighed Craven.

"But not for long. We will drive the French out of this country for good."

"What of the advance?" Thornhill asked.

"Masséna has moved masterfully through these mountains. We have engaged his rear guard at every turn, but so far we have not forced a confrontation more than a skirmish."

Thornhill got back to his feet as he hovered over the same map.

"He means to return to the shelter of Ciudad Rodrigo, where he will have a strong defence and time to recover his army's strength."

"I would meet the French in battle before he may reach that place," insisted Wellington.

"We do not have much time." Thornhill studied the map and could see positions marked out on it. He could see the enemy marked to a position on the far side of the River Coa at an area where it swelled out to the West, giving them a strong position across the hilltops like it was a fortress surrounded by a moat, "It will be no easy task."

"The French are weaker and more tired than our troops, Sir. I imagine they think themselves quite safe and secure there," replied Craven as he looked for himself.

"You would have us attack when they are at their strongest over this most difficult terrain?" Wellington asked curiously.

"I would have us do what the French least expect. We have fought a cautious war, and I imagine Masséna expects to retreat in good order whilst we take no chances, merely content to give ground. Our soldiers have been eager for a chance at the

French since the end of the year gone. The enemy are tired and starving. They are on the back foot and losing this war. They might be in a strong position geographically, but not in their minds and souls. Strike at them now. Give us a chance at them and let us show them what it cost to come here once more."

"If half of the officers in this army had your spirit, I cannot imagine how we could fail," smiled Wellington.

"I am willing to bet they do, Sir. I promised to throw the French out of Portugal, and I would not merely see them to the door, I would kick them out with both feet."

Wellington did not need to deliberate for long before he nodded in agreement, eager to deal a decisive blow after so much anxious waiting. He looked back to his map and how perfect the French positions were.

"If we are to succeed, we must strike them on all three sides. For resistance will be strong."

"Where do you want me?" Craven asked as he eagerly volunteered.

* * *

Craven approached a roaring fire as Ferreira chatted loudly with several comrades. He turned and rushed forward to embrace Craven, lifting him off his feet with excitement.

"I thought you meant to miss the fight!"

"I said I would see the French out of this country, and I will," insisted Craven as the troops were reunited.

"Tell me of Cairo."

"Maybe someday, but I would soon forget that place for a good deal of time," he replied wearily.

"And more importantly, we go into battle in the morrow," declared Paget as he joined them. Ferreira wrapped an arm around him, glad to see the young man's return.

"The enemy hold the hills over the Coa. Wellington will not attack that," replied Ferreira confidently.

"He will now," smiled Craven.

CHAPTER 17

"This is finally it, isn't it?" Paget asked, as clouds of his breath puffed out into the cold air. A thick fog covered the valley as rain poured down on them. They were the most miserable of conditions to fight a battle. Even so, everyone was in good spirits. For many of those formed up behind Craven were fighting not just for Wellington but also for the freedom of their country.

"How far to the Spanish frontier? How far must we push them, Sir?"

The officers waited in line, the Salford Rifles formed behind them, and the whole of the 1st Brigade of the Light Division at their front ready to march on the left flank of the French positions.

"Less than a day's march from here," replied Ferreira excitedly, as the moment he had been waited for was finally within sight.

An officer and his staff rode up past them, Sir William Erskine, the commander of the Light Division. He looked aloof, but not in a way which gave confidence in his focus on the task at hand. He appeared to have little hand on the situation, being surprised to even find his troops where they were.

"If only we had Crawford with us, Sir," whispered Paget.

"We will have to make do without him." Craven looked at the General with suspicion as he laid out his orders for the 1st Brigade to go on, and yet 2nd was left behind as the 1st marched on.

"What is he doing, Sir?"

"Nothing good, that's for sure."

"What do we do?" Ferreira asked.

"Stay here, but I would have eyes up there."

"We have not received orders," replied Paget.

"The regiment stays here. Moxy, Charlie, with me," he ordered.

"Where are you going?"

"I will not be blind because we are led by a blind fool. You have command, and you do whatever you have to do when it comes down to it, do you hear?" Craven ordered Ferreira.

He ran on with just two riflemen in support so that he could arguably not be in breach of his orders. They rushed on past the 43rd Regiment of Foot and the Monmouthshire light infantry, before reaching four companies of the 95th Rifles who led the Brigade with their Colonel at the head. As they approached the Coa ready to cross, they stopped to assess the crossing. Craven went straight to the man in charge who looked surprised to see Craven, although he recognised him.

"Captain Craven, do we really have the pleasure of your

company?" he asked with a smile.

"Yes, but not of my regiment, as they await orders."

"Major Beckwith," replied the commander with seemingly much admiration for Craven, despite them never having met.

"I much wished to have witnessed your advance at Talavera with my own eyes, but I heard from many who did."

"A victory I hope we can far surpass today, for the months which followed it were not a kind time," replied Craven.

Beckwith was no older than Craven. He looked fresh and eager, and a hundred times more confident and capable than the commander of the Division who he had just encountered.

"You would cross here, Sir?" Craven asked as he watched several of the 95th men test the water. It was deep and with a steep bank on the far side. Craven could not imagine it is where Wellington would have intended for them to cross. Yet with the thick fog they could not see an easier place, and there was no time to waste. The Major himself waded out to knee height, beckoning for the rest of the brigade to follow.

* * *

Paget was shaking with excitement, anticipation, and also frustration. He finally could not stand still any longer and began pacing back and forth across a tiny strip of ground just a few feet wide.

"We should be up there!"

"We have our orders, and that is final," Ferreira insisted.

"This is madness. The Captain will need us."

"And when he does, he will send for us," Ferreira replied calmly.

"I fear it might be too late by then." In frustration Paget looked to General Erskine. He was making light conversation with his staff and several cavalry officers, seemingly oblivious to the operations that were underway.

"This is the one, my dear Lieutenant. This is the day we kick the damn French out of Portugal for good. Be patient, for that anticipation you feel, we have been feeling and hoping on for months and years."

Paget came to a halt as he looked to the faces of the Portuguese troops behind them and what it meant to them. They looked ready to run into the fog ahead and not stop until they reached Spain.

"Our time will come soon enough," added Ferreira.

* * *

Craven waded through freezing water up to his armpits. It was a sobering experience as the whole brigade struggled on through. As they reached the far side, they could see the first French pickets. A few of the 95th men opened fire, killing two, but several others retreated as they cried out to alert the rest of the army to the British advance.

"The game is on, boys!"

Major Beckwith pushed through the water beside them, and they began to scramble up the slippery slope. Every man was now soaked through, and mud slicked up many of their trousers and sleeves. Their rifles and muskets were saved from the worst of the river but were still dripping from the endless rainstorm. Yet there was an enthusiasm and excitement amongst them all as they clambered up the hill before them. Several enemy pickets gave fire, but they were quickly on their way when they saw the brigade rushing towards them. The British troops stormed up the hillside as sporadic fire drove off the few French skirmishers from the top, and it was taken in no time.

"Form up!" Major Beckwith roared as company commanders of the 43rd echoed his commands, taking up positions on the precipice. The 95th continued on forward to harass the enemy. Yet swirling fog and rain gave little visibility. They watched as the 95th gave fire, but they could barely make out the targets they aimed at.

Beckwith was brimming with excitement as he walked the lines in front of the redcoats. He stopped beside Craven.

"We might have missed Talavera, but by God we will not miss Sabugal, hey, Captain? For this day will be remembered with the same glory!"

"Yes, it will," whispered Craven to himself, as he was determined to fulfil the promise he had made to his Portuguese comrades.

"Advance!"

But Craven did not move. He looked back towards the troops they had left behind before putting a hand on Charlie's shoulder.

"Get back there and tell Ferreira to get up this damn hill as fast as he can."

"What about our orders?"

"I don't give a damn. This is where the battle is to be fought, and I would not do it without them."

"Yes, Sir," she replied with a smile. She rushed off at such a pace her boots barely found grip in the wet mud, and she slid across the slick ground, vanishing over the edge of the hill and back into the fog.

"We are led by a fool here today, aren't we?" Moxy asked as he thought of the seemingly hair-brained general they had encountered back at their staging point.

"I fear it so, but there are many better men out here on this battlefield, and we will prevail."

They marched on beside the Monmouthshires down the slope to engage with the enemy who now knew a full-scale battle was inevitable. They moved to oppose the British as the two forces finally came head to head. Rifle fire still rang out from the 95th as they gave the French hell. With every step they took, the fog seemed to clear but not the rain. Soon enough they could see the size of the forge ahead of them, and it was daunting, and yet the size of the obstacle before them did not stop Beckwith who continued onwards.

They were soon formed up as the French began their advance, realising their numerical superiority. A volley of fire rang out from the thin red line, and a score of Frenchmen fell as they advanced. The redcoats began to reload, but as the rain quickly intensified to such a blistering degree, they could barely grip their ramrods as they were battered by the storm. The muskets were presented, and the command to fire given, but barely a half of the muzzles sent balls down range to the enemy. They in turn presented their own muskets to return fire, only to find their weapons equally unreliable in the horrendous conditions.

Beckwith quickly ordered the command to fall back to the hill position they had so recently taken, as the battlefield descended into the kind of swamp many would imagine Agincourt had been. For a while the two sides faced off against one another without movement. They waited for the horrific deluge of water to reduce as many worked to clear the misfires in their muskets.

The fog began to lift further, and the extent to which the British light infantry were outnumbered became apparent, none more so than to the French. Neither side could see how the rest of the battle progressed, but there was little sound of battle to suggest the British were making any significant assault. And so it all fell to the Light Division to bear the brunt of the French forces that seemed ferocious in their starved and emaciated state. Desperate men fighting in the most desperate of ways.

* * *

Paget could hear the ripple of musket volleys in the distance, and he could bear it no longer.

"We cannot delay any longer," he demanded of Ferreira.

They watched in amazement as General Erskine rode up calmly to the commander of the 2nd Light Brigade and watched as protests were made. They wanted to join the fight most urgently, and yet the General refused. He ordered them to stay where they were before galloping off with the cavalry towards the East.

"Where is he going?" Paget asked.

They could both see the disgust on the faces of officers and men of the 2nd Brigade, and yet there was nothing to be done for it.

"This is madness!"

"Salford Rifles, with me!" Ferreira went forward and led them on in a chaotic rush towards the river, causing a cheer to arise from the men of the 2nd Brigade.

Ferreira reached the water and ploughed into it before realising just how deep it was but would not turn back now. He took off his cartridge box and held it high above his head, along with his rifle as he struggled on through the gruelling conditions. He reached the far side to find the steep bank had been severely churned up by the 1st Brigade's advance, and he struggled to find purchase.

"Here!"

Up above he could see Charlie on a dry patch of grass. She was reaching down to offer him a hand. He stretched the muzzle of his musket up for her to grasp and levered himself up, hauling Paget up after him. A chain of troops helped one another out of the water, and they continued up the hill as a staggered worm of a formation, each man eager to join the fight as quickly as he could.

"What of 2nd Brigade?" Charlie asked as they rushed on together.

"They have been ordered to stand their ground."

"Why?"

"Because the General is a damned fool!" Paget cried out with no care for who heard him.

Ferreira smiled in amazement, and then so did Charlie, for the Paget they used to know would never have dared question their commanding officer, not even in private.

"He's not wrong. That old ass could lose us this fight," added Ferreira.

"Not whilst we fight," replied Charlie.

They stormed up the hill, panting for air as they struggled in the soft mud, and the rain continued to lash down upon them.

Eventually, they crested the hill and found Beckwith's troops reassembled atop the position. It was remarkably quiet as Ferreira roared for the troops to form up whilst he looked for Craven. He saw him smiling back at them as he approached.

"Where is 2nd Brigade?" Craven's smile soon vanished when he realised only the Salfords had come.

"Orders by General Erskine, they are not to cross the Coa," replied Ferreira.

"Why did they bother forming up for battle if they would not join it?" snapped Craven as he shook his head in disbelief and frustration.

"We shall just have to fight this battle ourselves," declared Paget with pride, as if glad to face the horrendous odds as they looked out towards the enemy positions.

The fog had all but lifted now, and they could even see the square towers and walls of the castle fortress of Sabugal, which might soon be engulfed in the battle to the North. But the lifting of the fog also meant every soldier could see the French outnumbered them three to one. The enemy skirmishers were forming up at a stone wall ahead of them, as infantry columns crossed it and began their advance.

"I see your boys have come to join the fight!" Beckwith shouted enthusiastically as he paced up to them with a broad smile on his face. It certainly hid the fear any sensible man might feel in the face of such odds, "Come and take your position, and let us show these French some cold steel!"

"Form up!" Craven led them into the line between the Monmouthshires and the 95th. They watched as the French columns advanced with much excitement, their drums beating loudly. Their officers advanced well ahead of their men,

261

swinging their swords about their heads and riling up their troops as they went forward. The advancing infantry were not the only threat. They watched French gunners deploy two howitzers on the opposed hill behind the advance. It was not long before they opened fire on the British position.

"We shall have to do something about those guns!" Beckwith held firm and watched the advance, "Hold fire on my command!"

They watched the enemy approach and endured the howitzer fire. The two guns ripped holes in their line but inflicted only few casualties, for how thin their formation was spread. The rain began to let up, as only thin sheets of drizzle peppered them. It was a welcome relief from the horrendous conditions they had fought through all morning.

"Nobody fires until I say so!" Beckwith ensured they all held their fire until it would give the most devastating of results as the French marched up the hill towards them.

"Ready!"

Orders were passed along the line as the hill now bristled with musket and rifle muzzles. The French were just fifty yards away.

"Fire!"

The first shots were enough to signal to the whole Brigade to fire. A vicious roar rang out, and the French lines were whittled down by withering fire. They briefly came to a standstill for how many they had lost.

"Reload!"

The company commanders did not even bother to relay the command. Every man knew what he had to do, as they all hurried to reload their weapons. Craven merely watched as he turned his focus to Amyn. The Mamluk now in his redcoat hurried to reload his rifle and was doing so at the same pace as the rest of them. The French drums continued to beat, and they resumed their advance up the hill.

"Aim!" Beckwith roared as they finished, "Fire!"

Another rippling fire devastated the front of the French lines. Many officers and NCOs fell, and once again their progress was halted as the British hurried to reload. The enemy were within thirty yards now.

"One more, boys! They won't take another!"

Craven could see the Frenchmen at the front begin to doubt their advance. He could see the fear in their eyes. It was the same loss of faith a swordsman had after being so utterly schooled in the opening pass of a contest that their heart was no longer in it, for they knew victory was impossible.

"Fire!" Beckwith roared for the third time.

The volley was horrific as it thinned the French lines, and many began to turn back. Even their officers struggled to keep moving forward. Beckwith could see his opportunity, as all of the British and Portuguese troops could, and he held up his sword high into the sky.

"Charge!" he roared without any preparation or warning.

The excited allied troops stormed forward from their hilltop position even as two howitzer shots smashed into the hillside around them. A war cry rang out from the British and Portuguese as they stormed down the hill with bare steel glistening as raindrops fell from the blades of bayonet and sabre.

Many of the French troops turned and fled. The few who remained were rolled over by the relentless charge of red and green jackets. They blitzed through the French advance and chased them back up the opposing slope, leaping over the stone wall. It forced the French gunners to hurry to try and move the howitzers, but they were too quickly overcome as the Anglo Portuguese troops overran their position. It caused the crews to flee with the rest of the infantry already in flight.

The charge came to a standstill past the guns. Cheers rang out as they watched the French troops flee, but it was soon muted as they saw thousands of French infantrymen approaching to drive them back from their newly acquired position. But worse than that was a cavalry force already advancing to attack them. Beckwith could hardly believe what he was seeing as their celebrations were silenced.

"Fall back! Fall back!"

They didn't need to be told twice as they heard the French infantry roar as they charged forward to join the cavalry. The British and Portuguese troops fled in a disorderly fashion, leaving the howitzers they had only captured a moment before. They rushed out across the open ground, desperately trying to escape the cavalry who increased their pace to a charge. The thunderous hooves of the horses shook the ground beneath the fleeing infantrymen. Craven reached the long stone wall where the French infantry had first launched their assault and leapt over it. He dropped down for cover and turned back to face the advancing cavalry.

"Come on!"

He called for his Salfords to rally behind the wall. Beckwith drew the rest of the brigade up as well, taking up position as if fighting from a castle battlement. The charging cavalry slowed as they approached the solid defensive line with bayonets. They finally came to a standstill as they drew out pistols and carbines to duke it out with those at the wall. It was as if two frigates had pulled alongside each other to shoot it out with one another, as balls struck the stone.

The British and Portuguese infantry reacted with glee to the fight turning in their favour. They reloaded, rested their weapons on the wall, and returned fire, knocking the cavalrymen from their saddles with ease. The cavalrymen struggled to reload from the saddle, as the infantry behind their stone defences quickly reloaded. They gave a second volley, leaving barely a single man still in the saddle. The last remaining troopers fled in horror at their losses.

The French infantry who had struggled to keep up with their cavalry now made their advance to find they faced another volley from the wall and an uphill battle. Their own fire had little effect against the stone, and the British returned another volley, causing them to falter and fall back once again.

Craven watched with amazement, having done almost nothing but watch the infantry fire volley after volley. They went back and forth over the same ground, but he now looked to the howitzers. A party of Frenchmen were attempting to recover one of them. He remembered the beating the Brigade had taken under the fire of the guns, and he leapt onto the stone wall, pointing his sword out towards the position.

"Are you going to let the bastards take those guns back?"

The troops around him roared with anger, as they watched him jump over and run on towards the French skirmishers, who were now broken with only a small number returning fire.

"Come on, lads!" Beckwith shouted as he encouraged the rest of the Brigade to follow Craven. They watched in awe as the Captain stormed towards the enemy with sword in one hand pistol in the other. He gave the enemy both barrels before knocking one musket out of the way and plunging his sword into the soldier's chest. He moved straight onto the next, as the Anglo Portuguese infantry stormed in to join the fight. They overran the French skirmishers and stormed on towards the howitzers. One French officer stopped defiantly ahead of Craven and directed a cut downwards towards him as he attacked, but he leapt aside, and the blade struck the mud. Craven cut back towards the man, but he staggered back, lifting his blade in time to cut Craven's blade away. It bought him enough time to regain his composure so that a duel ensued. Craven cut and thrust, and the Frenchman gave ground, taking each of the blows before returning a quick blow toward Craven's leg. He dropped his pistol down to parry the blow to free up his sword, which cut down onto the man's head. It cleaved his hat and knocked it from his head, but the headwear was enough to save him from harm.

Craven followed up with a thrust, but once more the officer cut it aside. Craven rotated his sword about the Frenchman's, dumbfounding him with a fast rotation, and driving the point up into his chest. He drew it out to let his body drop to the ground triumphantly, to find the troops had got ahead of him. They chased those trying to escape with the howitzers, striking down the last who remained to defend them. Beckwith roared to bring the Brigade to order, and they formed a skirmish line in the woods around the French artillery that had been claimed and silenced. Craven's comrades formed up around him.

They looked out towards the French lines. Yet more infantry formations were moving to dislodge them from their newly acquired position, as they had done so when taking the howitzers the first time. It was a hard thing to stomach after such a heroic effort to retake the ground in the face of such odds.

"Sir, look!" Paget yelled.

Behind them the whole of the 2nd Brigade were marching up to join the fight, in spite of Erskine's orders. The 52nd Light Infantry formed up on their right flank, a fresh-faced battalion ready to earn their spurs. The rain continued to pour down upon them, but the British resolve was now so robust not one soldier was willing to give ground as French infantry and cavalry moved against the wood.

"Load up, boys!" Beckwith ordered.

Craven watched as Ferreira took charge, barking his orders as the infantry fired volley after volley, but the French troops kept coming. The two sides exchanged fire as Craven waited for his opportunity to join the battle. As he reloaded his double-barrelled pistol, he watched with concern as French skirmishers and cavalry continually probed the lines of the 52nd Infantry, holding the right flank. The newly arrived troops struggled with the harassing tactics. Beckwith began to pace along the lines as he yelled encouragement and left it to his company commanders to keep up the fight.

"We do not relinquish these guns to the enemy again! Not again, do you hear me, boys!"

He rushed past Craven with a smile on his face, as if relishing every moment of the peril they faced. Volley after volley poured back and forth, as the bodies began to amass on both sides. The French infantry continued to pour forward in what seemed like insurmountable odds. The rest of the Anglo

Portuguese army was nowhere to be seen, and those defending the hill began to wonder if they had been left to hold off the entire French army by themselves. The French infantry finally gave one last salvo before directing their bayonets forward and charging against the wood, as they tried to drive the British and Portuguese from their positions. Yet not one soldier turned and fled in an unusual encounter where two strong infantry forces clashed with bayonet, and neither would give ground, as the two locked horns in a deadly combat.

Craven gave both barrels as the French troops stormed his line of Portuguese troops who had until recently been a militia force, and yet held their ground firmly in the face of a ferocious charge. He had never felt so proud of anyone as those who had volunteered to fight for him now gave regular troops the most ferocious fight of their lives. Craven threw down his pistol and took out his dirk. He leapt into action as he cut down a bayonet aimed at Sergeant Gamboa, thrusting his dagger into the man who had attacked him. Sword and bayonet went back and forth in a ferocious battle over the French howitzers, both sides fighting over control over them as if they were the most important things in the world.

The two sides pushed backward and forward, as ground was given and taken to be counted in yards, with no progress as neither side let up. Sweat and blood mixed with the continuous rainwater as the mud began to run red with blood. The British troops fought for the position with everything they had in such a determined defence that no matter what came at them would move them from the hilltop.

Amyn stormed into the French troops like a berserker, slashing in a stunning display. It unnerved the French troops with his rapid long drawing cuts so close to his body he was right up against the French troops. Birback looked in disbelief and rushed on to join the Mamluk, as if to not be outdone, or at least join in the fun he was having. Charlie followed him, eager to join in the bloodletting as she remembered the loss of her husband and the rage it had forged within her mind and body.

The Salfords drove forward with ferocity as they cut and thrust. For every step of ground they drove the enemy back, they'd see more advancing to join the contest of the hill, which both sides fought over with an unwavering and deadly drive to succeed.

The last of the mist finally lifted, and again showed how small the British light infantry force truly was compared to their French counterparts. Another infantry force moved to push them from the hill, in what no commander would ever believe could be held off. The Anglo Portuguese force was holding the hill now running with blood and with bodies piled high.

Beckwith watched as French infantry marched towards their unguarded left flank, as he had no answer. Everything he had was engaged with the enemy, and even all those who had come to reinforce them were now just as embroiled in combat as his 1st Brigade was. He paced along the line, just as Craven stumbled back into him with a bloodied face where a cut had opened over his left eye.

"Captain, we face the whole French army, and we need a miracle. Tell me you have one!"

Craven struggled to find an answer as they heard the beat of the drum. They looked down the slopes to the North to see the last of the fog on the River Coa lift. A British infantry division was advancing to support their unsupported flank.

Cheers rang out from the Light Division as they saw the infantry in the centre open fire and drive the French from their exposed flank. Beckwith looked back. The French before them were beginning to falter after an hour of contesting the howitzer position, which had seemed of little consequence at the opening of the battle and was now the chief objective of the entire battlefield.

"Go on!" Paget roared excitedly as he watched the infantry advance and maintain fire. They swept the French from the battlefield, and it became clear to everyone that the tide of the battle had been turned.

"Look at that. I am swept up in it, just as I have read. I am part of the Craven story, and we have done what Craven does. Speak to them, Captain, speak to them!" Beckwith yelled enthusiastically.

Craven was amazed to hear it, but he did as asked, and climbed up onto a fallen tree to see out across the lines. Many of the Frenchmen paused to hear him just as the British and Portuguese did.

"You see that!" Craven pointed to the East, "Over there is Spain. Everything we have fought for and everything you have sacrificed for it, it is just there! It is there for the taking! Take it!"

There was an awkward silence and pause in the fighting as exhausted troops contemplated what he had said, and what energy they had left in their bodies. Finally, a cheer rang out from Sergeant Barros, and the Portuguese troops led the call. They cheered in support of the dream of regaining their country after waiting out an arduous winter in hiding behind the lines of Torres Vedras. The hope of claiming their country back had seemed an insurmountable task, and now it was so close they could taste the sweet victory. The British infantry began to join in the cries of excitement as if they had already won the battle; to such a degree many of the French troops took a few paces back. It was as if they thought the enemy were close to beaten, and now realised how far they were from success.

"Push them back to Spain!"

Ferreira ran forward with his sabre in hand, leading them as he fought to make his dream a reality. He smashed down the musket of one Frenchman with his own rifle, caving in his head with his sabre before anyone had responded. That was all the rest of them needed to see as to join the charge. Craven and the Salfords stormed forward with the rest of the Light Division rushing on in support as the French lines gave way and began to retreat in disorder.

"Charge!" Craven roared as Beckwith looked to him, and they ran on together.

Craven cut from one side to another against the infantrymen who held against them as a wave of red and green jackets stormed out from the woods. They smashed into the demoralised French lines. They were even more fatigued than they were, after the Anglo Portuguese lines had mustered one last great surge of energy to do what they had dreamed of doing for more than a year. The French infantry turn their backs and ran for their lives.

The Anglo Portuguese forces advanced across a vast area as all elements of Wellington's army made it across the Coa. They gave pursuit to a demoralised French army who were finally beaten in open battle. Those giving pursuit knew they had finally overcome a great army of Napoleon in open battle. They chased the enemy until exhaustion across slick mud and the most horrific of ground for several hours until finally they came to a halt, knowing their work was done for now.

Craven drew in a deep breath of relief as he looked out across the frontier towards Spain, watching the French army flee. He watched as the enemy formed an admirable rear guard, but it only delayed the inevitable as the French army was chased out of Portugal and out into the Spanish frontier.

Officers cried out as they tried to rally British troops to pursue and end the Frenchmen, but it was to no avail. Every single soldier was exhausted and had given even more than they imagined they had to give. Craven stopped and watched gleefully as the enemy crossed over to the Spanish frontier. Every soldier under his command revelled in the delight of seeing one of Napoleon's great armies flee across the border, after having entered the nation in their third attempt to pacify the seemingly modest country that had stood against the most feared man in all the world.

The Salford Rifles stopped beside him as they realised the pursuit was over for now. They had all done all that they could do, despite knowing the war was far from over. Ferreira was the most emotional and came to tears as he watched the French troops leave the border of his country he had never seen until becoming a soldier. Even Birback was relieved for it to be over. The exhaustion set in for all of them. Many were battered and bloody, and they had left a great number of their comrades in the mud behind them.

Beckwith stepped up beside Craven without any of his staff, having pursued the enemy as an individual in the chaos that had followed. The army ground to a halt, having no energy left for the pursuit as horsemen rode up beside them. They initially ignored them until Thorny called out.

"Fine work!"

They looked around to see Wellington amongst the party. They had galloped up to see the progress for themselves, and Beckwith almost dropped to his needs in apology for ignoring their commander.

"Fear not, Major, for the Light Division has won this battle, and I am in eternal gratitude for it. Had Napoleon led their armies, we should have lost this contest, and were it not for the Light Division, we would also have lost it. And not for General Erskine, a fool of which I cannot imagine is still able to wear the uniform of England and not feel shame!" Wellington roared.

"It is not without Captain Craven and his Salfords I could have achieved it," admitted Beckwith.

"Do not credit Craven for too much, or his head will get too large, and I would not give this victory to a single man," replied Wellington.

"This wasn't mine." Craven looked out at the army who had formed before him.

"Nonsense, you were as fortifying as a French Eagle to the men of the Light Division!" Beckwith replied.

Craven smiled, but he shook his head as he went on. "They barely saw me, but you did, Sir," he declared to the Major, "You believed in this story which has been woven, and I will not deny its power, for it can be a powerful thing."

Beckwith did not know how to take it, as he looked at the fleeing French forces. They were soaring across to the Spanish frontier and ensured Portugal was finally re-taken, as had been the ambition for several years.

"If not a great hero, what are you, Captain?"

"I am a fighter, the same as every man under your command, who fought with every bit of heart and strength as I did this day," admitted Craven.

"And now?"

"Bring these men food and wine, for I have never known any who have deserved it more."

Beckwith nodded in approval.

"And you shall have it!" Wellington declared without hesitation.

Beckwith sighed with relief through utter exhaustion. He begged his leave of the General, but Craven stayed and looked back with an accusing glance.

"You have something to add, Captain?" Wellington asked in earshot of Majors Spring, Thornhill, and several of his staff.

"This victory, it was not as you imagined it, and not even as you even believed possible?" Craven asked bluntly as not even a General would dare ask of the commander of all the forces in Portugal.

Wellington seemed to hold back for a moment, considering his options, as if he had never experienced such a situation, finally accepting that he had a responsibility to the man who had given him so much. He took a deep breath and slowly spilled all.

"This battle here on the edge of this fine country was to be the great battle which ended it all, and yet it was very nearly the very opposite," he admitted.

"But it was not, and here we are, Portugal is saved."

"I have a great debt to the Light Division, but it is not owed to General Erskine, is it?"

Craven shook his head.

"What would you have of me, Captain? I owe much to the Light Division and to the 1st Brigade, but especially to you, so what would you have of me?"

Craven smiled, as he knew the position of power that he was in. The situation as a gambler he so rarely ever experienced.

"The wine of your staff, give it over to the men of my command and the 1st Division of the Light Brigade. For never have men been so deserving."

"You shall have it, and more," replied Wellington sympathetically.

* * *

"Look at it, is it not a sight to behold?" Ferreira asked as a fire was sparked up. They were still watching the French infantry retreat over the border into Spain.

Cheers rang out in support as they celebrated the enemy leaving their border. Paget and the rest of Craven's Blades joined the Portuguese troops as they toasted the defeat of the enemy, only to roar louder as Craven entered the scene to a huge applause after a triumphant battle. They gathered about the commander of their small and obscure unit, falling silent as they waited to hear him speak. He took a deep breath and prepared himself to address them.

"I promised you I would see the French from this country. For many here it is your country, and I can only imagine what that must mean. We have done it. You have done it. Tomorrow we shall drive the French through Spain and all the way back to France, but tonight we celebrate all we have achieved. Drink now, drink to Portugal, and to victory!"

Some of them clapped but not all understood, and yet they watched as Ferreira approached a cart and poured himself a glass of wine from a barrel. He held it up as he cried out to his comrades, and they finally understood the success they had achieved that day.

"To Portugal!" Craven roared.

None of them heard his words as they poured and spilled wine, but it didn't matter anymore. They all celebrated the same cause as he held up a cup amongst friends.

"To victory," he smiled.

THE END

Printed in Great Britain
by Amazon

87544504R00161